RYAN MICHELE

CHALLENGED

VIPERS CREED MC #1

Challenged (Vipers Creed MC#1) by Ryan Michele
©Ryan Michele 2016

Editor: C&D Editing (http://cdediting.weebly.com/) &
PREMA Romance (http://www.premaromance.com/)
Proofreader: Silla Webb (http://tinyurl.com/AlphaQueensBookObsessionAS)
Cover Designer: Pink Ink Designs (http://www.pinkinkdesigns.com/)
Formatting: Pink Ink Designs (http://www.pinkinkdesigns.com/)

ISBN-13: 978-1530562930

ISBN-10: 1530562937

This book contains mature content not suitable for readers under the age of 18. This book contains content with strong language, violence, and sexual situations. All parties portrayed in sexual situations are over the age of 18.

This is not meant to be a true or exact depiction of a motorcycle club. Rather, it is a work of fiction meant to entertain.

CHALLENGED

PROLOGUE

*M*Y HEAD FILLED WITH A CLOUDY, dense fog that I couldn't shake. Even with my eyes open, a filmy haze covered them, making everything blurry. Voices were muffled, as if I were under water, sinking. I thought I recognized one, but I couldn't tell for sure.

Too hard to think.

I attempted to pull my arms up, but they were immediately halted by something. The hard, cold, heavy attachments clinked like metal. Even straining to move them, my muscles were so weak, so lethargic I couldn't. I tried my legs, and the same thing happened.

A hard surface pressed against my back as the cool air of the room cascaded over my skin, my nipples, my stomach... Oh God, was I naked?

I opened my mouth, wanting to scream as deep panic set in. Unfortunately, nothing came out except air. Even that took more effort than I had in me.

Placing the pieces of the puzzle together, I couldn't make heads or tails out of anything.

Heat at my side had me turning in that direction, only to see a fuzzy, black figure. I squinted then blinked, trying to get the focus to come back, but nothing.

Not a damn thing.

"Hello, darlin'. Welcome to hell."

ONE

TRIX

A LUMP GATHERED IN MY THROAT settling like a rock, hard and brutal, sucking the wind out of me. My hand slightly twitched as I dialed the number I never in a million years thought I would call. I switched the phone to my other hand in an effort to shake out the trembling, because nervousness wasn't an option. Trix Lamasters would not turn into some twit who couldn't think straight over one phone call. Being a shrewd businesswoman, I'd learned from the best not to let shit get to me, how to compartmentalize things and deal.

I swallowed hard, moving the lump from my throat to settle into my gut like a boulder. As I focused, my breathing evened out. The thick steel in my spine could handle anything life threw at me, including this call. Including the man who would be on the other end of the line.

The green button stared back at me, my finger hovering over it. Then I pressed it and pulled the phone to my ear just as it started ringing.

One ring … two … three …

"What?" was barked through the phone line with a male's voice tainted by harsh impatience.

"Can I talk to Cade? Shit." I stopped myself. He wasn't Cade anymore. I needed to remember that a lot had changed. "I mean, Spook. Is Spook around?"

Silence.

"Hello?" I pulled the phone away from my ear, looking at the bright screen, making sure the call hadn't dropped. Nope, the little numbers in the corner were still counting away. I pressed it back to my ear, waiting a few beats.

"Who wants to fucking know?" His tone turned gruffer, almost as if he were a protective watch dog of Cade's, and nothing or no one got past him.

Watch dog or not, I wasn't about to get eaten.

"This is Trix Lamasters. I need to speak to him."

More silence, not even a breath or noise in the background.

"Hello?"

His voice came over the line right as I intended to speak again. "Stop fucking saying hello. I'm here."

Hell, maybe someone pissed in his Wheaties this morning, his attitude having nothing to do with me. Or maybe it was just him.

I slapped my hand to my forehead as the word *dumbass* rang in my mind.

"Sorry, I thought the call dropped." Now I apologized to the rude man? *Get a grip, Trix.*

"What do you need with Spook?" The guard dog didn't give me an inch. Nevertheless, he didn't need to know my business.

I needed a diversion.

"Can you just get a message to him to call me?"

"Babe, either tell me what you need, or nothing fuckin' gets to him." His tone turned flat and resolute.

"Fuck," I muttered then heard him chuckle. The damn man needed a bone before he played. Asshole. "An employee of mine has been seen at your clubhouse. I need to talk to her."

"Call her," he quipped.

"She doesn't have a phone," I retorted, feeling the fire burn in my veins.

"Not my problem," the man sneered. From his attitude, I knew he would have no problem hanging up on me right now, never telling Cade I needed to talk to him.

Good thing I dealt with assholes on a regular basis.

"Look, the bitch owes me money." Anger raced through my body. I let it be heard through each clipped word.

He let out a deep laugh that was almost intriguing if he weren't a jerk. "You may as well kiss that cash good-bye."

My pride had other ideas.

"Fuck no. I want what's owed to me." I sighed, needing a different tactic. "Look, can you just give Spook my name?" He would either call or he wouldn't, but maybe that would get the dog to want to nose around. Maybe curiosity would get him to spread my name at least.

"This is gonna be fun. Hang on." The man must have covered the mouthpiece with his hand, because everything he said was muffled except for him calling Spook's name. That, I could hear clearly. My adrenaline spiked at the thought of Cade coming on the line.

"Yeah?" a voice I recognized from my dreams said into the phone. The deep, raspy tenor had grown over time and slithered down my spine all the way to my knees, giving them a slight tremble. It took only one word to make my stomach flip.

Fuck, I knew this was a bad idea, but I wasn't that girl anymore. He would not have power over me. I wouldn't allow it.

I paced my small living room, needing the movement to get my knees back in line.

"Cade? It's Trix Lamasters."

"First, the name's Spook. Second, who?"

That one kind of stung. Alright, more than stung. It tore another hole in my already battered heart was more like it. The asshole didn't even remember me, but what did I expect, being one in a sea of many? There was absolutely no reason I would have stood out to him.

"We went to school together," I tried.

Silence.

I rolled my eyes to the ceiling, hoping divine intervention would give me the gift of patience or a gun. Neither came.

"Whatever. I get you don't remember me, but you have one of my employees there. I need to talk to her. She owes me money, and I need it back."

"Trixie Lamasters." I could hear the devilish grin as his words snaked over the phone. Not going to lie, my pussy quivered.

No one called me Trixie anymore, because once upon a time, he did and I had loved it. After he abruptly left my life, taking the one thing I could never get back, I refused to let anyone call me by that name. Never again would I allow the hollow feeling that name represented to seep through me. Now, hearing him after fifteen years, the vault of memories opened wide, something I did not want to happen. I didn't want to feel, yet each recollection of the past bombarded my mind.

"Long time."

I paused mid-step as a flash of younger Cade hit me. Shaking my head clear, I continued to pace through my living room.

"Yeah, very long. Anyway, you have a woman there by the name of Nanette King. Can you hand her over to me?"

I wouldn't let the smoothness of his voice draw me in like it had all those years ago, reducing me to a pile of teenaged mush. *Strictly business*, I told myself, because business I could handle.

"How do you know she's here?"

"I had her followed, and it led to you."

I guessed he didn't like the fact that I had found her that way, judging from the muttered curses that followed. Each word made me smile. I had a payroll of people who worked for me now, and some little twit-fart would not run off with my money. That wasn't how I operated my business.

Nanette had fallen off the radar. Cade's club happened to be the last place she was seen; therefore, I had to call him. I may as well have strapped zip-ties around my wrists, locking them in place.

"First, if she's at the club, there's a reason. Second, bitches here don't go by their real names, so I don't know if she's around, because I don't know a Nanette. Third, you come to the clubhouse, and we'll talk."

Business was business, but my heart spiked at the thought of seeing him again.

Cade's club, Vipers Creed MC, had been in Dyersburg for years. Even before I came into this world, their presence had been well known. This town had tales, but these days, the Vipers were mostly known for Creed's Automotive where they made custom bikes and cars in their own little world located on the outskirts of town.

I'd hoped to avoid a meeting since I couldn't see any point to it. I wasn't in the mood for a high school reunion. The past needed to stay there, locked up tight.

"I'll describe her to you. Tell me if she's there, and I'll send someone over to get her," I declared, trying to veer him from this path.

Negotiations were something I excelled at. There had to be an arrangement that suited us both, one we could manage over the phone. It would be the best course of action. The less contact I had with him, the better. I could have Ike, one of the bouncers at Sirens, pick her up. Win-win all around.

He chuckled, and my body went on alert because of the slyness in it.

"Babe, you don't get how this works. You want something from me that I have, bring your ass here, and we'll discuss it. Tomorrow night, seven." Silence.

This time when I looked at the screen, the number fifty-seven blinked rapidly. He'd hung up on me.

"That arrogant piece of shit!" I growled, tossing my phone to the couch where it bounced on the cushion.

I should have known he'd still be a dick. Some things never changed. Guess I was going to meet up with Cade after all.

I completely ignored the slight tremor that thought caused.

DURING THE ENTIRE DRIVE, I berated myself for giving the money to Nanette in the first place. One stupid decision started this path, one I could have avoided if I'd stuck to my rules.

Nanette's eyes were anxiously cast to the floor of my office as she rung her hands together absently.

When she didn't talk, I prompted, "Speak." It sounded like a command I would give a dog, but at times like these, when people wouldn't get on with their shit, it was deserved. I had shit to do, and she obviously needed something.

"I need to borrow five thousand dollars," she said in a surge.

I leaned back in the leather chair behind my desk, my brow raised as her eyes looked everywhere but at mine. Nervous? No, she was damn near petrified.

I waited out the quiet for her eyes to meet mine, the fear coming across loud and clear.

When they did, I asked, "For what?"

I wanted to hear her out, because if she had problems, I needed to know whether those problems would blow back onto Sirens. It was always about the business.

"The bank's gonna foreclose on my house if I don't come up with the money by Friday." *Her eyes filled with moisture.*

While I wasn't a cruel and heartless bitch, this wasn't my problem. She was a grown adult and needed to handle her own problems, including money to pay her bills.

"No," I answered firmly. *"You can go now."*

Nanette's face turned to dismay as my answer rolled around in that head of hers. Her skin paled, her nose twitched, and she swallowed hard, as if not to puke. She began to say words; only, they came out as sounds of mumbled breath as she lost her composure.

I held up my hand in an effort to stop her choking rambles. "Stop trying to talk. Listen. I'm not a bank. I'm not an ATM machine, and I do not run cash advances. You need money, you work for it. That's how the world goes round."

"Please," she started in a rush. *"I'm taking care of my dad. He's sick, and if I lose the house, I'll have nowhere to make sure he's okay."*

"Not my problem." *This was one of the reasons I closed myself off from the people around me, only letting a small few into my tight-knit circle. I had heard so many sob stories over the past five years running Sirens that not much penetrated the thick wall around me.*

"Trix, I'll pay you back every penny with interest. Please. You're my last hope. My dad has lung cancer, and it's progressing quickly. All my money goes to his treatments, and because of that, I got behind on the mortgage. I just need an advance on my checks. I'll work extra shifts, and come in whenever you want." *Her words strung together like a melody, and fuck me, I felt her panic.*

She continued, "He has no insurance, so I'm paying for everything out-of-pocket. It's bleeding me dry. I don't know what else to do." *Tears rolled down her face. Judging from* her body language, which I had learned from the best how to hone in on, the bitch was telling the truth.

Fucking hell. I didn't want to feel it. I tried to push it back. The businesswoman inside of me screamed, 'No fucking way!' while the woman inside of me was proud of how Nanette took care of her father. Was I really going to do this? Shit.

"Twenty-five percent interest to be paid in full six months from now."

Nanette's eyes lit up in shock. "Really?"

"That's six thousand two hundred fifty dollars in my hand six months from this date. A fucking day late, I'll make your life a living hell." I would, too, finding every way possible.

"Okay," she said, swiping away the remnants of her tears, a flash of relief snaking into her eyes.

I folded my hands, placing them in front of me. "I'm not fucking around, Nanette. These are the terms." I pulled out the gun from the holster attached under my desk, setting it on the hard wood. Her eyes widened. "Every last penny in six months," I reminded her. "You sure you wanna do that?" It was the only out she would get if she agreed.

She nodded her head then spoke, "I understand. Six months, sixty-two fifty in your hand."

I put the gun back in its holster, my warning as clear as I could make it.

"Out. I'll have the money for you by the end of your shift."

My damn pride would not let this go. The bitch owed me a lot of money. I wanted it back. I wanted her. If that meant I had to go into unfamiliar territory with a guy I did not like, so be it.

"Oh, my God, he's coming this way," my friend Beth practically screeched.

I hit her arm, trying to get her to stop embarrassing the hell out of me, as the hottest guy in school walked our way. Most considered him on the bad boy list, and damn if that didn't send my heart a flutter.

His eyes locked on mine. I couldn't stop staring; he had some sort of trance over me.

Those blue eyes held mischief and intrigue.

"Hey. How you doin'?" His voice was deeper than most of the other boys in school, making him seem older and more mature.

"Fine," I responded, my nervousness coming through on that one word.

"Wanna go out?" he asked as my heart squeezed. The hottest guy in school had just asked me to go out with him. Holy fucking shit.

"Sure," I replied as calmly as I could.

"Cool. Meet me at six at Regan's."

Regan's was a local diner hangout that we all went to regularly.

"Okay."

He winked then turned, striding off.

Beth's wide smile mimicked mine as we closed our eyes and did a silent, little, open-mouth scream. I had a date with the Cade Baker.

As I pulled myself out of my thoughts, my breath hitched at the monstrosity in front of me: huge cinderblocks stacked one on top of the other, higher than my two-story house. The ends looked like princess parapets with sharp points in the roof. Windows all around them provided a view of every direction. At closer look, I noticed men standing inside them, their eyes trained on me. I felt like I was going into a war zone instead of a motorcycle club.

I rolled up, stopping the SUV at the closed gate to the entrance.

Unease whispered around me due to the heavy security. Who in the hell were they protecting in there, the fucking president?

A large man built like a stubby Mac truck with a goatee and light brown hair came up to my window, his eyes covered by black glasses. I hit the automatic button to lower my window, waiting for it to clear all the way down.

"What can I do for ya?" he asked, bending into the window with a smirk on his face. He made no qualms about looking down the front of my shirt at my ample cleavage. I hadn't worn the shirt for that purpose, but I had very few shirts that didn't show off the girls.

I snapped my fingers three times in quick succession, and his eyes met mine. "My eyes are up here."

"But down there is just as fucking good." He licked his lips as lust blazed off him.

Men, they were all the same: Booze, bitches, and boobs.

"I'm here to see Cade." Dammit, I needed to stop that. *Cade* wasn't his damn name any more, but separating the two came as a challenge. "I mean Spook. He's expecting me."

"Fuck, boss man always gets the prime pussy." He groaned in a way that suggested this type of occurrence was routine, an idea which I pushed out of my head as soon as it entered.

I arched my brow. "No one gets my pussy but me," I combated, tilting my head just a touch.

I told things like they were and didn't back down from a fight or a challenge. That being said, I had also learned how to cut my losses and get the hell out of a bad situation. Burly man here would not intimidate me.

"Doubt that one." He nodded to one of the guys in the tall tower, and the steel gate slowly started to open with a loud creak in front of me. "Have a good time, and when you're done, come find me."

"No, thanks," I murmured, driving away from him with no intention of searching him out ever.

The wide area felt vast, almost like a whole city block. I had lived in Tennessee all my life, so of course, I'd known of the Vipers Creed. Everyone did. However, to actually see their compound, to be in their space, unnerved me. There was an aura of power that I felt down to my bones, causing me to fight back a shiver.

Vipers Creed MC had bought an old army compound many years ago. The structure on the outside reminded me of the classic war movies I passed by on television. Inside the gates, though, looked nothing like the starkness of the outside.

Several buildings outlined the space. An enormous structure looked like it had two, maybe three, levels to it. I assumed that was the main building, because several smaller concrete structures surrounded a large courtyard with bright green grass and a fire pit off to the side. Some actually looked as if they were homes with plants and flowers around them. It seemed homey, comfortable in a way, like a family lived here and took care of it.

Off to the far left sat Creed's Automotive, with several hot rods and a few bikes lining its parking lot.

A spot near the larger building came into view. I parked my car, turned off the ignition, and then sat back in my seat, giving myself a moment. I did this before every business meeting just to make sure I got my head on straight. Too bad this meeting had to be with Cade. If rumors over the years served me right, he was the president of Vipers Creed. The two guys I had talked to confirmed it with the *boss man* bullshit.

People changed a lot over time, going different paths, some good and some not so good. I wasn't a judge, jury, or executioner in this scenario, but I had to wonder, with all the security, exactly how much Cade changed from the boy I'd known all those years ago. Did his life happen to be so dangerous that he had to be behind cement walls with guys guarding them? And if it were that dangerous, why would he choose this life?

I wanted to bang my head on the steering wheel. It didn't matter. I was here for one reason and one reason only. I should have found comfort in the knowledge that the meet was business, but it didn't come.

With a heavy sigh, I opened the SUV door then hopped down to the blacktop. I pulled my shirt down, readjusting myself and making sure the girls were covered. I'd gone simple, wearing a pair of ripped jeans, a blue V-neck top, and flats. I loaded myself up with silver on my wrists and a couple of chains around my neck. I didn't do much with my hair besides run the brush through it. I liked having my chestnut tresses fall in thick waves down my back.

"Hey, mouse," a man with a bald head and a tailored beard said from my left. Black sunglasses covered his eyes, and his lips were lifted into a sexy smirk. He wore a leather vest, which had a *Secretary* patch on it, over a dark blue T-shirt. He was attractive in his own unique way.

Mouse was a strange greeting, but I went with it.

"Hi, I'm here to see Ca—Spook," I told him, lifting my hand to block the penetrating sun that my sunglasses had no chance of hindering.

"I bet you are." He chuckled, running his hand over his beard as he appraised me.

I should have felt heat from his intense stare, but I didn't. Okay, maybe a flicker if I was being honest with myself. I knew how I looked, considering I saw myself in the mirror every morning.

My body drove some guys crazy because I had an abundance of tits and ass. I understood that. It was even flattering that men found me attractive. At the moment though, I didn't need his appraisal or anyone else's. I just wanted to get this shit over with. In and out. Wipe my hands clean of Cade again.

"Can you tell me where he is?"

The bald man walked closer, holding out his arm with a crooked elbow like an usher would do at a wedding. I smiled. It was cute, especially from a burly man like him. I placed my hand in the bend of his firm arm.

"Let me show you to him," he said.

We began to walk, and all the while, the heads of the guys sitting in the courtyard area turned and whistles erupted. I ignored the noise, falling into step with the man.

"Thanks," I told him with a pat on the arm.

"Anything for the boss man."

While I didn't know Cade's life, I had some assumptions. I watched the television shows about men in motorcycle clubs and all the havoc they raised. I didn't know if they were actually true, but at least I wasn't going in completely blind. I did know they had a hierarchy of power, and the men had to ride Harley's. Other than that, I only knew what the TV shows told me.

Who am I kidding? I was pretty much clueless.

The man chuckled deeply. "So, what's a hot piece like you coming here for?"

When he asked the question, I looked up at him. Lines sprinkled around his eyes and lips like he'd ridden his bike in the sun for hours. His face matched the tanned color of his head. It wasn't a look, though; it was him.

A small grin played on his lips, catching my attention. I didn't know if he already knew the answer to his question and was playing me or if he actually was being inquisitive. Once again, I rolled with it.

"I have word one of my girls is here with you. She owes me money, and I want it."

He opened a solid, steel door, and we walked into darkness. I ripped my sunglasses from my face as the low hum of the newly turned on lights illuminated the room. The scents of stale booze, cigarettes, and sex permeated the air like a thick haze. I knew those three smells by heart because I smelled them every day. They were my livelihood, the reason I had stepped foot in Cade's world.

"This way," he said, pulling my arm.

I followed him into a wide open space. Tables were scattered throughout with chairs at each of them. A long bar sat on the other side of the room with loads of liquor, looking like it could give me a run for my money in comparison to the one I had at Sirens.

I felt kind of strange holding this guy's arm without knowing his name, so I asked.

He lifted his shades to the top of his head and stared down at me with eyes the color of the ocean. They weren't blue, and they weren't green. They were both, and they were breathtaking. I got sucked into them momentarily.

"Stiff."

"Stiff?" I questioned as he walked me through the space and down a long hallway. What in the hell kind of name was Stiff?

Pictures hung on the wooden planked walls, but at the pace we were going, I had no time to look at them without stumbling over my own feet.

He chuckled. "Yeah, mouse. You stick around, and I'm sure you'll find out why." He winked then stopped us in front of a wooden door. With his fist, he banged loudly three times, shaking the pictures on the wall next to the door.

"What?" barked a voice from the opposite side. Even with the wood between us, with that one word, I felt my body instantly awaken, wanting to pull toward the sound.

"Someone here to see ya," Stiff yelled back.

"Nice intercom you have here," I murmured.

Stiff chuckled.

Little did I know opening that door would change my life forever.

TWO

TRIX

THE DOOR FLEW OPEN, SENDING MY hair back in a whoosh.

"She ..." Cade's words stopped, a smile appearing on his alluring lips. "Well, hello there, little mouse." He looked over at Stiff approvingly. "You brought me a present?"

There was that damn word *mouse* again. Did I look like a rodent or something?

Stiff snickered, and I stiffened. Did he think I came to play?

"No," I said with every bit of authority I had, pulling my arm away from Stiff's. "I know I'm a little early, but we have a meeting at seven."

Cade's eyes lit with recognition. *So now he remembered me.*

"Trixie?" He sounded dumbfounded.

God, the years had been good to him. He was hot then and sexy as hell now. The universe was a nasty son of a bitch. He had the same jet black hair as when we were kids except longer, almost down to his shoulders, with a slight wave to it. The five o'clock shadow around his lips looked like maybe it could be a ten o'clock, instead. The dark scruff only added to his defined features.

His eyes. God, his eyes. They were the things that got all the girls, including myself, to bend to his will. Blue, but not just any blue. No, his were a cobalt blue that reminded me of a beautiful Japanese vase I had seen once.

Venturing down farther, I saw a leather vest with a black T-shirt underneath, spanning across his wide chest. The patch of *President* was in bold white letters stitched into the fabric with several other patches lining either side. His bare arms may not have had fabric covering them, but they were covered from wrist to under his shirt with tattoos that looked intricate in their design. Bottom line, I thought he was gorgeous in school, yet now, sexy hot didn't even cut it.

I blinked, coming out of some sort of daze, and pushed my confidence back into gear full force. "It's Trix. We have a matter to discuss," I reminded him as he stared, looking at me from the tips of my toes to the top of my head, appearing to take me in just as I did him. "And you checking me out isn't solving that." Hypocrite? Yep, that's me.

Sure, my perusal of him was perfectly fine, but him … I shook my head. Smartass mouth rears its ugly head.

"May not be solving your problem, babe, but the view is spectacular." His voice was even deeper than over the phone. Sexier. Smoother. While good over the phone, it happened to be so much better in person. *No, Trix. Get your money and get the fuck out.*

I tried not to let the blush creep up my neck. I knew it did, anyway, from the heat I felt.

I cleared my throat, gaining his attention back up to my eyes from my tits. "Nanette. I want her so I can get my money."

My traitorous body had other ideas besides the cash, though, as arousal punched me in the gut. I willed the quivering between my legs to stop with little success. If anything, with each second I stood in this man's presence, the feeling became more intense. Thank Christ I wore a padded bra, or my nips would be raging through my shirt.

His pink tongue swept across his plump bottom lip. I watched each painstakingly slow inch. Brief flashes of that tongue on my body, my neck, my breasts coursed through my head. It took me back to a time when his touch encompassed me.

I broke my gaze from him, not wanting to go there. I couldn't go there.

"Why don't you come in?" he coaxed, opening the door wide in invitation.

Stiff chuckled beside me, and my gaze swung to him.

"What?"

His head shook almost knowingly. I wish I knew what he did.

"Nothing. In ya go." The heat from his hand on the small of my back guided me into the room, him following.

Two men sat in front of a large wooden desk with stacks of papers, a computer, and a phone on it. Their eyes instantly prowled me up and down, my skin prickling from all the attention.

I received male perusals at work all the time. Sirens was a strip club, after all. Regardless, from the way their eyes scanned, I felt devoured. The room was filled with a dominance that pulsated off the walls, bouncing around the space in waves: darker, rawer, more … manly. The smell was heady. It wasn't just the two men; the power came from all four of them together in this confined space. I didn't know if I should be intrigued, turned way the hell on, or if I should run for my life.

"Who do we have here?" asked a man with pepper hair streaked with salt and a matching beard that fell down to his chest. Even sitting in the chair, I barely had to look down at him, which set me on edge.

"This is Trixie," Cade announced.

My head snapped his way. "Cade, I told you my name is Trix," I ground out, surprising myself with the retort. Normally, I kept myself in check, but being in this man's presence short-circuited my brain, making my sass go on a rampage.

A deep laughter filled the air. "Yeah, *Cade*," salt and pepper man teased while the other two men hid their amusement. Still, they did nothing to hide the fact that they were openly checking me out.

"Damn, Spook, how long has it been since someone called you that?" said another man who had light brown hair that was totally unruly, like he'd either just gotten out of bed or had run his hands through it a thousand times.

Cade's eyes were on me, penetrating me with his glare. He took a step forward, and I took a step back, unsure if that look boded well for me.

My awareness of my surroundings came into focus, and unfortunately, I saw the room only had one door. The window was high, so I wouldn't have enough time to get out. Internally, I sighed. I knew better than to leave home without my gun.

"I fucking told you, the name is Spook." His body pulsed, and I felt it down to my core, shaking me a bit. However, I held firm, not moving another inch or flinching. My stubborn ass wouldn't back down even if he could hurt me. Truth be told, he'd already hurt me worse than anything physical he could manage.

I held up my hands, palm up, surrendering, my bracelets falling down my arms and scraping my skin. This was his rodeo, and I needed him calm to get what I needed.

"Sorry. To me, you're Cade. That's how I remember you. I don't know you as Spook." What happened to the boy I'd been with in high school? This definitely wasn't him. No, he was all man now, and I needed to be mindful of that. "I'll do my best to call you Spook. Where in the world did Spook come from, anyway?"

The men in the room didn't hide their full-out laughter. Cade cut them off with a furious glare.

"That's a story for later. Out," Cade barked at the men, who got up, shaking their heads, and left the room just like Cade had ordered. The door shut with a click that echoed in the space like a loud warning buzzer.

As his eyes penetrated mine, it took every bit of steel in my spine to keep myself from shrinking under their intensity. I met his stare, not giving an inch. The heat in the room crackled like electric wires were attached to both of us, drawing us together. I tried to fight the pull.

"Trixie." The one word rolled off his tongue, but not in the anger he gave the guys when he ordered them out of the room. This was different. "I'll always be your Cade."

My stomach fell. I stood here fifteen years later, in a room alone with Cade. The boy who had crushed me as a kid, who still had a fucking hold on me that I hadn't been able to let go of and we were only feet apart. Thoughts of the past bombarded me.

His penis touched my entrance while he hovered over me. I could feel the tip pressing into my unused body. I closed my eyes as Cade pushed in farther, pain searing through me as he moved. I said nothing, though, trying to hold back the whimpers in my throat. Sex was supposed to be fun and feel good, or so my friends had told me. This didn't. Not at all.

"You're so fucking tight, so fucking good." His words felt nice, giving me the extra nerve I needed at that moment to keep going. I wanted to make him feel good.

His body stilled, his eyes slicing into mine with confusion then understanding. "Fuck, you're a virgin," he growled.

I blushed. I had kept it from him. I'd heard the stories of him from other girls. I knew he wasn't a saint, and for once, with Cade, I wanted to be a sinner. He made me feel, and I needed that, craved it.

"Fuck, why didn't you tell me?" Intensity flashed in his eyes, scaring me a little.

"Just do it, Cade," I told him as he looked perplexed, like he didn't know what he should do.

I grabbed his hips and gave them a squeeze, answering the silent struggle in his head.

"It's gonna hurt," he told me, closing his eyes like it would pain him to see me hurt. It only made me care for him that much more.

We had been seeing each other for six months. He hadn't pressured me into sex, but I knew he wanted this. I wanted this. I wanted to be closer to him in any way I could.

"Do it," I repeated, and then he thrust inside me hard.

The pain shot through my gut, and I cried out, unable to contain myself.

Cade put his hand over my mouth to muffle my wail. "Trixie, you can't scream."

I knew I couldn't. We were at a party at one of his friend's houses. No way would I let anyone see me like this.

I got control of myself as he pushed in and out of me, the pain not leaving. If anything, it became more intense. I kept my eyes closed, hoping the pain would subside.

"God, you're so fucking good. Most beautiful girl I've ever seen."

Tears welled up, both from the hurt and from his words.

"This feels so damn right. So damn perfect."

Unfortunately, I wanted it to be over so the pain would stop. Either Cade didn't notice I hurt, or he didn't care. I hoped for the first, but I wouldn't stop him. No, I had wanted this for too long.

After several more drags in and out of my body, Cade stopped while I continued to fight back the tears. His face fell into the curve of my neck between my ear and shoulder. He glided his nose across the sensitive skin as his breath came down hot, tingling all over.

I could feel his breaths deepen as if he were breathing me in. He gave me a soft kiss there before he rose, his eyes on mine.

"You okay?" His concern relieved me, but I didn't want to sound like a naive idiot.

"Yeah, I'm good," I lied, just wanting him to get off me so I could go to the bathroom. Surely, there was more to this sex thing than just this. Right?

I didn't get a chance to find out with Cade, because after that one night, after he held me for hours, whispering stupid shit I never should have fallen for, he left. He hadn't left school or life. No, he left me. I was a ghost to him. Not even in existence. He looked right through me. I turned out to be nothing.

The burn from the moment hit me hard. Some things in life you didn't get over. They shaped you into the person you were today. That was one of those moments for me. The moment I swore I would never let any man get in my head again. Including now.

Head in the game, Trix.

"Listen Ca—I mean, Spook. I just need Nanette. Then I'm out of your hair." I moved to the side of the room as he went to the front of his desk, leaning his ass on it and crossing his arms and ankles. An air of confidence beamed off of him. I had to admit, the appeal wasn't lost on me. He was hot, the dangerous, live-on-the-wild-side kind of hot. His legs were so damn long, his muscles flexed under the worn jeans. I felt the heat in my body rise.

His eyes bore into me with a wicked promise gleaming inside of them. His promises meant nothing to me, though. They were only words where he was concerned.

"This Nanette, you say she works for you?"

"Yeah, at Sirens. She dances and is a waitress."

His brow quirked, and a slow, easy smile came across his lips. "You own Sirens?"

He said the words like he didn't believe me, and it caused my hackles to rear up.

"Yes, I've owned it for five years."

I built Sirens from the ground up, working my ever-loving ass off to make it a success. My father taught me a lot about business, and I took all of that knowledge and turned it into something I loved. I proved to myself that I could do it. Sirens was mine through and through, and it was also the only reason I'd put myself through the aggravation of seeing Cade again.

"Well, isn't that something?"

My temper rose at his condescending tone. "What the fuck does that mean?"

He held up his hands, palms out. "Put in the claws, wildcat."

I would do no such thing while he talked about my business. I refused to take any shit from anyone about it.

"It just surprises me," he finished.

I crossed my arms over my chest, mimicking Cade. His eyes flickered to my now exposed cleavage, and another smile creeped on his lips. I rolled with it, tapping my foot in angry bitch pose.

"And why would that be?" I snapped.

While he stroked the whiskers on his face, my mind instantly wondered what they felt like. Were they rough or soft? Would they leave a burn in their wake?

I stopped tapping my foot as I got lost in the thought.

"Back in the day, you were so innocent, so mild mannered."

Oh, hell no.

All thoughts of his beard flew out the window. "We are not talking about the past, Cade. I want Nanette, and then I'm gone."

He lowered his voice. "Trixie, I've been in that pussy of yours. Let's not pretend I haven't."

I rolled my eyes and looked up to the ceiling, hoping for patience. When it didn't come, I aimed my glare at him. "You were in it *once*. One time. Don't mistake that for knowing anything about me now." Then I felt the urge to be a bit catty. "You better remember that taste, because that shit won't *ever* happen again."

"Didn't know I was offering," he said as a comeback, pissing me off. He'd always been good at comebacks. Damn him.

I let out an exhausted breath and released my arms to let them hang at my sides. "Can I just get Nanette so this shit can be done, and I'll be gone?" None of this was getting me anywhere, and I had already been here much longer than I cared to be.

He uncrossed his ankles and rose to his full height. His demeanor was a strong, all-encompassing aphrodisiac. *Shit.*

He licked his bottom lip again then ran his hand over his beard. It shouldn't have been seductive, but it was, so very much. I really needed to get the hell out of here. "One thing you need to know, Trixie."

I ground my teeth at the name yet kept my mouth shut. My body may have been pulsing for him, but I refused to give him any more.

"You want something from me, something from my club, you pay for it."

"How much?" I asked, figuring by the time this was all over, I'd only get about four thousand back of the six plus Nanette owed me.

I kicked myself in the ass for giving in. All of this was my own damned fault, but at least I could take it out of Nanette's ass by putting her on a pole.

"See, that's the thing. There are three ways you can pay." Great, now I had choices.

I raised my brow for him to continue.

"Cash, blood, or pussy."

"Well, blood and pussy are off the table, so again, how much?"

He snickered. "Same smartass mouth I remembered."

My blood boiled. *He remembered?* You've got to be shitting me. He didn't even remember my name on the phone. I didn't need to hear any of his *memories* from then, because he clouded and tainted all of mine.

"Ca …" I shook my head. "Spook, seriously, I need to get to the club. You want a cut of the money? How much?" Unease crept in hard and fast. *Bad idea.* I should just leave and be done with it. Forget the six grand and forget Cade. Forget all this bullshit. Two things stopped me, though. One, no one stole from me; and two, my personal assistant Jett's words rang through my head: "*It'll set a precedence with the other girls, and they'll think they can walk all over you.*"

Fuck, I couldn't let it go. I needed to call Nanette out on her shit. Dammit. I hated when my back felt up against a wall.

"Too bad your cash isn't good here. So that leaves you with two options: blood or pussy." He grinned that sexy half-grin of his that made my panties damp. Fuck, it had gotten better over the years. He'd damn near perfected it. "Since I don't want your blood, I'll take your pussy."

"I'm not fucking you." Confidence wailed in my voice. Not happening. The only way he'd get between my legs was if he used the jaws of life. Been there, done that, and burned the fucking T-shirt.

He moved so quickly he came at me in a flash. I pressed my back to the door, his body so close his chest brushed my nipples through my shirt, sending tingles of warmth throughout my body. He placed his hands on the door at either side of my head, boxing me in. I tried not to panic as I evened out my breathing.

"Trixie," he whispered, the scent of cigarettes coming off his breath, and I inhaled deeply.

I looked directly into his eyes, resting my head on the door and giving myself a slight bit of distance. Just as I suspected, his eyes pulled me in, the warmth and lust rolling around them in a swirl. I tightened my hands into fists as they itched to reach up and touch him. I fought the urge with everything I had.

"Thought you were hot fifteen years ago." My stomach curled at his declaration. "Now, baby, you're off the fucking charts."

I tried to move farther away, but he wouldn't allow me. So, I retorted, "Thanks, but that doesn't get me my cash back."

He pressed his hips against me, his steel erection hard, long, and thick against my stomach. My pussy quivered. The whore wanted him badly. The arousal kept gaining and gaining on me even when I tried to make it stop.

"I fucking want you," he practically growled.

I hated to admit it, but I wanted him, too. However, I had too much respect for myself.

"That's nice, but get over yourself."

"I'm gonna be over you, under you, and in you," he vowed, easing down to my lips.

I tilted to the side as his lips touched my cheek. Not going to lie, the small touch, along with his sexy as hell words sent fire racing through my veins. I wouldn't show it to him, though. Hell no. Regardless, his words—holy hell, I'd never had a guy talk to me like that, and judging from the slickness between my legs, my body liked it a whole hell of a lot.

He shifted back, the sexy, panty dropping grin back in place.

I looked him square in the eye and said, "You couldn't handle me, Cade." Sparks exploded in his eyes at the use of his name. "I'm all grown up now. Your sly smile, magnetic eyes, and words aren't gonna get me to spread my legs for you. You had your shot and blew it. That's on you."

The grin grew full-out, almost as if I were throwing down a challenge, and he liked it. Absolutely not my intention.

"I get what I want, Trixie."

"It's Trix, and as much as I want my money, this"—I pointed between the two of us in the small space I had—"ain't happening."

Cade pressed me harder to the door, his entire masculine body against mine, squeezing the air out of my lungs. I could feel the definition of his chest on my breasts, his thick thighs against mine, straining and rock solid. I gulped, holding on to my bravado with all my might. I could do this. I *would* do this.

He brought his hands to the sides of my face, and in a flash, his lips came down on mine hard, wet, and insistent. I put my hands on his rock of a chest to push him away, but he didn't budge, even with my hefty shove. Instead, his lips devoured me. This wasn't a kiss. No, it was more like a brutal, all-consuming, and rough assassination of my lips, and I gave every bit of it back to him.

My tense body began to soften as Cade's magical mouth moved, and his tongue flicked across mine. The taste of tobacco blossomed on my tongue, and instead of pushing him away, I caught myself clutching his shirt, instead.

Snap out of it! I broke the kiss unexpectedly, ducked down under his arm hastily, and backed away from Cade to the other side of the room.

"Get back here," he demanded.

I shook my head and swiped my hand across my swollen lips, the smell and taste of him warping my senses.

"I'm not doing this. I'm not some fucking whore you can have just because I need something from you. No offense, but I'll forget about the damn money and deal with the bitches at work. What I will not do is fuck you."

I'd find another way to get Nanette. I already had Ike get his guys on the case. I trusted Ike with the job because my father gave me the skills to know how to make judgment calls on people. Another reason why the circle of people around me stayed so small. The only thing he'd learned so far, was Nanette's father had passed away and the bank was close to taking the house.

Cade's eyes flared. I didn't know if it was from anger, annoyance, or both. Regardless, I didn't want to stick around to find out.

"I'm leaving," I told him as he stood near the door, his hands in fists at his sides. "Move out of my way," I ordered.

He didn't budge. *Asshole.*

"Come by tomorrow."

The randomness of the sentence caught me momentarily off guard.

"What?"

He crossed his arms over his massive chest, the tattoos bulging from his muscled flesh, sending another shot of lust through my system. Why the hell did that one move seem so damn hot to me?

"We're having a party tomorrow. Your girl shows up, you can take her."

I raised my brow, placing my hand on my hip, not believing him for a second. "Just like that?" I asked, snapping my finger on the last word.

He chuckled. "We'll go with that."

I knew he wasn't going to. If I came back, he'd do anything and everything in his power to get me in his bed. I didn't want to test my willpower when it came to him. Any other man, not a problem. But not with Cade. I wouldn't tempt it.

"Let me out." I refused to reply since he wouldn't like the one I'd give him.

He pointed at me with a look that said I had better listen. "Your ass better be here tomorrow at eight. If it's not, I'm coming to find you. And, baby, I won't be happy."

I jutted my hip out, my hand on it. "And I was put on this planet to make sure that *you're* happy?" I laughed, but it was in no way humorous. "No, Cade. Now move out of the goddamned way," I ordered.

He opened the door behind him and stepped to the side. I surged toward it, needing to get the hell out of his space and get some fresh air.

He grasped my arm, halting me, and I turned toward him. "I mean it, Trixie. Your ass better be here tomorrow. That's the only fucking reason I'm letting you go right now. Eight."

He crushed me to him like I weighed nothing, smashing his lips to mine and taking me with vigor, sucking the air from my lungs. The hot, deep, and quick lick of his lips as he pulled away, followed by his sexy growl, had me feeling like I was floating.

I shook my head to clear the fog. Cade smirked, the same one he had when we were kids, and it still made my belly flutter, but the man who had just kissed me was nothing like the boy I had known.

I turned and hightailed it out of there with absolutely no intention of ever stepping foot on this ground again. And I needed a damn shotgun to shoot every damn butterfly that entered my belly.

Rushing down the long hallway, I went into the first big room I entered earlier. Stiff and the two men who had been in Cade's office sat at a table, each nursing a beer. Their attention immediately came to me.

"Where's the fucking fire, mouse?" Stiff asked.

I stopped, turning toward him. "Do I look like a fucking mouse? Do I have four legs or a tail? No, I don't. Don't fucking call me that again." I glared, and Stiff's rumbled laughter filled the space.

Yes, he actually laughed.

"You're feisty." He didn't know the half of it. "Spook not give you what you need?" He wiggled his eyebrows in suggestion. "I can help you out."

Stiff was attractive—don't get me wrong—but seriously?

"No. I have a vibrator at home that never lets me down. Y'all have a nice life." I flipped my hand up in the air dismissively as I stomped out of the door. I needed to get to work.

THREE

SPOOK

"**W**HO'S THAT?" BEN ASKED FROM NEXT to me, pointing to a girl bending down at her locker.

Her jeans hugged her ass, but the oversized shirt covered it when she rose. Her wavy, brown hair came just below her shoulders, the light reflecting off the waves, giving it a soft shine. Then she turned around, and her bright, wide green eyes connected with mine. She clutched her books to her chest, hiding herself from me.

In that moment, I felt something slam into my chest. It curled around and tightened its hold on me, gripping with everything it had. I couldn't put a name on that something, though. I'd never felt it before, especially never from a look.

"What's going on?" Jaden came up beside us, taking in what we were looking at. "Ah, Trix Lamasters, freshman."

At his words, a girl came up to Trix, and she turned away from me. The smile she gave her friend knocked me on my ass. Beyond gorgeous. It lit up her face like nothing I'd ever seen. And not to be cocky, but I'd been around a lot of girls. None of them, not one, had the pull this girl did.

Trix didn't look back as she walked off.

That moment started my infatuation with the girl. Obsession was more like it. That day also marked the beginning of the end, an end I forced because it had been best for her and best for my club.

In life, hard decisions sometimes have to be made, and pushing her away like I did was shitty of me. It was also one of the hardest things I've ever had to do in my life.

She hadn't done a damn thing wrong, but it was best for me to ignore her and pretend she didn't exist.

But damn, now little Trixie Lamasters was back.

I watched her tight, sexy-as-fuck, round ass swing down the hallway like a fire was chasing her. Her tits had practically burst from her shirt, and the outline of her curves made my fucking mouth water with the urge to lick every fucking inch. Not to mention, her green eyes could pull any sane man into their depths.

What got me the hardest though, was that she didn't fucking back down. No, she stood toe to toe with me, throwing that hot as hell attitude my way. Who'd have ever thought she would come back into my life after fifteen years? Fuck, not me.

Now she was hotter and sexier than even my imagination could have conjured up in all these years.

I had played as if I didn't recognize her name on the phone when as soon as I heard the name, I knew. I knew the eyes, the smile, the smell of strawberries that seemed to follow her wherever she went—*her*. I'd in fact, kept my eye on Trixie over the years, having others stay far in the background, watchful. I knew she owned Sirens—fuck everyone did. However, it sure was fun getting a rise out of her when she assumed she and her business weren't even a blip on my radar.

Fuck, my dick turned to concrete after being pressed up to her heat. I adjusted it, but it brushed against my jeans, not helping a damn bit.

I moved down the hall, following her, and listened to Trixie have an exchange with Stiff. One thing was for certain: she was a fireball. Good thing the guys around here liked that spitfire attitude, or she'd find herself bent over a knee, getting her ass spanked. That actually sounded like a perfect idea.

Her taste lingered in my mouth, not sating the craving I had for her. If anything, it made the want almost painful.

When the door to the clubhouse slammed shut, I stepped out into the main room.

"Spook, don't tell me you're losing your touch," Stiff teased.

"Fuck off." I grabbed a chair, turning it around before sitting my ass on it. Then I rested my arms on the top and lit a smoke, inhaling deep.

"New mouse?" Bosco asked jokingly. He knew the answer. He'd been around forever, all the way back to when my old man ran the show. He hadn't cut his hair or beard since then, either; I swear it.

I shook my head. "Nope. She's no mouse."

Stiff chuckled. "Could tell just by looking at her."

"So, that's *the* Trixie Lamasters, huh?" Bosco asked, the knowing look blaring through his eyes. Everyone who was around back when my father was president knew of Trixie. Not only because of me, but from club business, as well.

"Yeah, that's her."

Bosco whistled low. "Damn, brother. What's she doing coming around here?"

"Do we have a mouse by the name of Nanette?" I asked.

House mouses were the women in the clubhouse who were free reign in the fucking department. They came and went as the wind blew. Only three mouses had stayed for the past full year, and countless others had come and gone. And I'd fucked them all. They were willing, and it was their duty. They kept us happy, and we provided them protection, at least for the most part. If they had some messed up shit that we didn't want blowing back on the club, we kicked their asses out. I didn't need that kind of heat just for pussy.

"Not that I know, but I don't really know their names," Stiff said, pulling up his beer bottle and taking a swig from it. "You need me to find out?"

"Yeah. If she's here, I wanna talk to her. Trixie said the bitch owes her money. Need to find out what the hell's going on." I turned to the bar. "Lee!" I yelled, and the scrawny-ass, pimple-faced kid came from behind the door. He needed a dermatologist immediately. He was new, prospecting for the club. I needed to figure out his loyalty first, then I'd tell him about his fucking face. "Beer," I called out.

He nodded and brought it over to the table then disappeared. *At least he's learning*, I thought as I inhaled off my cigarette.

"So, Trix thinks this Nanette is here?" Boner, my vice president, asked.

We called him Ben through school up until he got his road name. He knew more about Trixie than anyone else here.

"She says she has someone who saw her here, which means Trixie has eyes. I don't like that shit." It pissed me off my guys hadn't seen it. I didn't like anyone in my business, even a sexy as hell woman. No fucking way. That shit had to stop immediately.

Boner ran his fingers through his hair. I swore he was going to start losing it if he kept that shit up. "Want me to have Dawg look through the tapes?" Dawg was in charge of keeping eyes and ears open at all times. Everything around Vipers was videotaped.

"Yeah. He finds something, you tell him to come to me with that shit, so I can rip his ass for it." I never liked being blindsided with shit, and if he didn't catch some asshole lurking around, he'd hear it from me.

"On it." Boner looked over at Stiff. "You on Nanette?"

"If she's here, I'll be over her."

We all chuckled as Boner and Stiff stood.

"You sure she doesn't wanna be a mouse?" Stiff asked hopefully, though the slight smirk told me he was fucking with me.

"Yes. And no one fucking touches her, or their ass is mine." I stood and threw back the last of my beer, slamming the bottle on the table then stomping out my smoke. If another man touched her, I'd go ape-shit.

"Already staking claim?"

"Fuck, wouldn't you?" No man with eyes would say any fucking differently.

Stiff smiled. "Fuck, if you didn't, I was on that shit."

My face grew serious. "You spread that shit wide. She's coming here tomorrow. Any motherfucker touches her, he deals with me."

"You got it, boss man."

Bosco cut in, "You sure you wanna do that?"

Was I sure I wanted to fuck her again? Fuck, yeah. Second chances rarely came, and when they did, if you didn't grab them, you were a fucking fool. I was no fool, but I couldn't reduce it to just that.

"Yeah," I answered, the pull I'd always felt for Trixie hit me like she had a fucking rope around me. Being in her presence merely tightened that shit, bringing it all back to the surface.

"You know what that's gonna mean, right?"

I rolled that over in my head. I knew I'd open up old shit, shit she didn't know about. I weighed it against my need for her. Fuck, even thinking of being with Trixie came with a slew of consequences I could bring on my club. But I couldn't let her leave again without finding out if she had what I needed. My gut told me she did, and it hadn't let me down yet.

"Let's see where this shit goes first."

Bosco nodded and headed out.

"Get Rip in here!" I called out from my office door in the garage. I had two offices, one for the business and the other for the club. Lately, I'd been spending equal time in each.

The demand for custom bikes and cars had grown by leaps and bounds. Mostly, it was from weekend warriors, but what the fuck did I care when they were paying top dollar for that shit? The bikes and cars made up a bulk of our income. It was also one hundred percent of my aggravation.

Nevertheless, Vipers Creed was my family, my soul. I worked my ass off to clean up the mess my asshole of a father left the club in. He lost track of the main goal of the club—family. Instead, he had gone with greed and ended up getting a bullet to the head by my hand, something I had zero remorse for.

I knew Vipers was more than what he had thought. We weren't perfect, and our teeth weren't sparkling white by any means, but we were a family.

"Yeah." Rip came into the office, wiping his hand on a rag so greasy he smeared more than he wiped off.

I waved the paper in my hand. "Parts order on the Morrison bike. It's still not filled out."

He held up his finger and left the room. I tossed the paper onto the desk and waited.

Two seconds later, Rip came in with a paper of his own, handing it to me. Thank fuck.

"Good. Don't let there be a next time."

He lifted his chin in recognition as I looked over the form. Unlike my father, I was very hands on when it came to keeping track of everything. I didn't place the order—I had a guy for that—but it damn sure went through me first. I wanted to know exactly what money moved through the business and the club. This ensured everything stayed in line. I would not lose control like my old man had.

A knock came to the door, then a sing-song voice said, "Spook."

I put the paper down. "Hey, Mom."

She walked in, her head held high with all the confidence in the world. She always dressed in all black with some type of huge belt around her waist. She'd been the top ol' lady for quite some time here, putting up with my father's shit. When I took him out, she lost her place, but she was still family.

I stood from my chair and walked around the desk. She came right into my arms and wrapped them around me. "My boy, how are you?"

I pulled away and stepped back behind the desk. "I'm good. You?"

She waved her hand in front of her. "Oh, fine," she lied. I could always tell when she didn't make eye contact with me.

"Don't lie to me, Mom."

She let out a huff of air. "I need an advance."

Boom, and there it was. Money. She always needed fucking money. She got a small cut from the club because I didn't want to leave her high and dry after taking out my father. We gave her enough to live on if she wouldn't keep blowing it on stupid shit.

"You're gonna need to get a job if you keep this shit up." My bluntness came with everyone, my mother being no different. Besides, I was getting fucking sick of this game.

She put her hand on her hip, and I raised my brow. "I took care of you—"

I held up my hand to shush her, and she complied.

"I don't wanna hear that shit. I'm thirty-three years old. Been running shit for fifteen of them. So don't bullshit me." I fell into my chair and raked my fingers through my hair. "How much you need?"

"Only four thousand."

My mouth dropped. Never had she come to me with that big of a number. A few hundred, okay. She even asked for a thousand once. But four k? Fuck no.

"What in the fuck did you spend that kind of cake on?"

She twisted her hands, showing me how nervous she was. Good. She should be nervous. This fucking shit was coming to an end. "I sat in on Fox's table."

Now I ripped both my hands through my hair and looked up at the ceiling. There would be no help there, but if I looked at my mother, I would jump over the desk and strangle her ass.

"I lost."

I glared. "No fucking shit. You lost, and now he wants his money. What are you gonna do if I don't give it to you?"

I knew exactly what Fox would have her do. He ran tables in the back of his bar and made serious bank off them. He also ran girls, and that's exactly how he'd have my mother pay—on her fucking back.

"You have to," she said, her eyes wide like she realized for the first time I was contemplating letting her pay off her own debt.

"I don't have to do shit. *You* put yourself there, not me."

"But—"

"Don't." I remained stern, and she tensed. "When do you have to have the money?"

"Next Friday."

That gave me six days.

"Leave. I'll call you and let you know what's decided."

She started to say something, but I gave her my don't-fuck-with-me stare, and she walked out, her shoulders slouched slightly.

I slammed my hands onto the desk. "Fuck," I growled out.

She'd been getting worse and worse. I'd been letting her ride. But this ... I couldn't let this slide. Worse off, I'd have to bring it to the table, and we'd all have to vote on it. I had my own cash to pay for it, but no matter how it got paid, it put the entire club on Fox's radar.

I felt like a selfish bastard for not coming right out and helping my mom for all of about five seconds. I'd bailed her out so many times over the years. She needed an ol' man to keep her ass in line. Until then, I needed to figure out what the hell I was going to do with her.

EIGHT-THIRTY AND NO TRIXIE. I smiled to myself as I lifted the beer bottle to my lips. The cool liquid flowed down my throat.

"What the fuck you smiling about?" Boner asked from beside me with a house mouse draped over his lap.

I cocked my head toward her. "Worry about her, not me."

"On your knees," Boner ordered the woman, who fell to her knees in the grass like a pro. "Undo my pants and suck me until I come." The mouse followed the instructions to a T. "Now, what the fuck are you smiling about?" He threaded his hand through her hair as he stuck his dick down her throat, the crowd of people a distant memory for him.

"Fucker," I stated, and he moaned. "Fuck. Come see me when you're fucking done." I moved away from the scene, adjusting my hard dick. One might think that seeing his brother get a good face fuck wouldn't be a turn on, but they would be wrong. That fucking shit was hot.

"Hey, Spook," a woman purred from next to me as I walked toward the fire pit, lighting a smoke.

I turned to see Stacy who'd been here for a few months. We'd had our share of go-arounds. She was pussy—not pussy to write home about, but pussy, nonetheless.

"Hey."

She trailed her hand down my sleeveless arm. "Need me to help you out?" she cooed.

While I was rock hard from witnessing Boner, having Stacy take care of me didn't have the same appeal. All that kept flashing through my head were thoughts of Trixie: her tits, her ass, and that fucking long-ass hair. My dick grew harder, and Stacy smiled, thinking she had caused it.

"I can see you do." She moved her hand to the button of my pants, and I stepped away.

"Did I say you could fucking touch me?" I growled, causing her eyes to widen.

"I'm sorry. I—"

"You nothing. Go find someone else before I kick your ass out."

She scurried away, fear in her eyes.

I was being a dick, but she touched without asking, which was a rule of being a house mouse. They couldn't touch unless a brother invited them to. No exceptions. I should kick her ass out right now, but I had other shit on my mind.

Stiff sided up to me. "Damn, Spook, you alright?"

I glared at him, and he held his hands up in surrender.

"I'll be back." I tossed the beer bottle in the garbage bin and smashed the cigarette on the ground with my boot as I moved toward my bike.

Trixie was bringing her ass here on the back of my fucking ride … right after I spanked it.

FOUR

TRIX

I WASN'T STUPID. CADE'S EYES YESTERDAY told me that he meant business, that he would come and get me. He also knew where I worked. It was why I took the night off and let Jett run the show. I didn't do it often, but I knew Sirens was in perfectly good hands.

I wasn't a social person, keeping mostly to myself. Over the years, people had proved to be unreliable, so I only trusted myself fully. Jett, though, had been with me for three years and was my closest friend.

Cade didn't have a clue where I lived. I wasn't listed anywhere, always afraid one of the patrons would come to my home. I only had a few people who knew where I lived, and I liked it that way. You just never knew who you could trust anymore.

As soon as I left his office, I'd decided I was never going back. Ever. I would get Nanette some other way.

I was done with Cade's domineering attitude. I mean, who in the hell did he think he was? No way in hell was I digging up that shit. *I'm gonna be over you, under you, and in you.* I scoffed, the sound echoing in my living room. *Hm, I'm so sure.* One heartbreak from him in my lifetime had been more than enough.

I called in Ike, my bouncer, bodyguard, and all around go-to guy at the club. He'd increased the watch on Nanette's house, which she surprisingly hadn't lost yet. He'd already checked her bank and phone records before I'd gone to Cade. So far he'd gotten nowhere, but he was still keeping tabs. It was only a matter of time.

My cell rang from the table, snapping me out of my thoughts. Happy for the reprieve, I grabbed it.

Taylor Calling.

In a husky, sexy voice, I answered, "Hey there."

"Hey, yourself." Taylor's deep voice reverberated through the line. "You working?"

I smiled, moving over to the couch and sitting down. Taylor was a booty call—no other way to describe it. He was decent in bed and didn't want entanglements, same as me. We'd been hooking up every so often over the past five or six months. It wasn't regular by any means, and it was only for the sake of having a warm body to get off on. I'd allowed him in my home a few times, but he'd only stayed for an hour or two max and then took off.

"No, night off."

"Really?" he asked in surprise, which was justifiable since I *always* worked. It was usually later in the night when we hooked up or during the day, yet it wasn't unusual for him to call and set it up.

"Really."

"I'll be over in twenty," he said, not giving me a chance to say anything else before he hung up.

I flew off the couch, running into the bathroom where I brushed my teeth and checked my makeup. After running the brush through my hair then adding a touch of lip-gloss, I checked my body, making sure I smelled good. I ran into my bedroom, changing into a pair of white booty shorts that showed off the cheeks of my ass. Then I tossed off my bra and put a camisole on, hiking up the girls to their full potential.

After seeing Cade yesterday and feeling his lips on mine, I'd been running fiery hot. My vibrator couldn't fix it. I should know; I tried … twice. I got off, but I wasn't sated in the slightest. I could still feel Cade's body pressed against mine, his heat surrounding me. I hoped Taylor could help me banish the Cade memories.

I spritzed on perfume then took another look in the mirror. Curves were showing, and my waist looked good.

You sure you wouldn't rather Cade be the one coming over?

I frowned in the mirror, shaking my head. Where in the hell did that thought come from?

No Cade. Taylor. He'll make it good for you.

I finished by putting lotion on my legs, smoothing it up my thighs.

When the doorbell rang, my head snapped up, tilting toward the clock. *Damn, those twenty minutes went fast.*

I rushed to the door, throwing it open to find Taylor standing there with a wide smile across his impeccable face. He was a bit of a pretty boy, not much edge to him. He was clean cut with blond hair and deep, brown eyes and absolutely no facial hair, or hair anywhere on his body except below his waist for that matter. He wore dark jeans and a button-up, short-sleeved shirt in green. It gave his brown eyes a greenish tint. He held a jacket in his hand.

"Hey there, beautiful." He strode in the door, not wasting time. He tossed the jacket, wrapped his arm around my waist, and picked me up as I slammed the door shut.

I wrapped my legs around his body as his lips came to mine. Only, the spike of excitement I normally got from his kiss was diminished greatly. It didn't burn me like the kiss from last night. That kiss had taken my breath away. Taylor's kiss was too sweet, too … nice.

Stop it, I chastised myself, kissing him back. *I will not think of Cade*, I fought with myself, *only Taylor.*

He sat on the couch so I could straddle his thighs, keeping his hard dick beneath my core. I moved my hips back and forth, gaining groans from him. My pussy decided it was time to wake up, enjoying the friction.

He cupped my breasts and squeezed them, but I needed more. I needed …

Stop it!

Bang, bang, bang.

The loud noise at the door had me breaking the kiss from Taylor and turning toward it on a gasp. Through the side window, I could see a brooding Cade. His arms were crossed over his wide chest and his demeanor … Well, pissed off didn't even cut it. His eyes were almost glittering as they stared back. He was furious.

"Fuck," I groaned, getting up from Taylor.

"What the hell?" he said, adjusting his dick as I pulled down my shirt.

"Old friend. Let me get rid of him."

I turned back to the door and walked slowly toward it. On the other side, Cade's face contorted in a fury that sent a tremor down my spine. His jaw ticked, his mouth set in a tight line, while his eyes were narrowed into thin slits. The anger came off him in waves, even through the thick door.

Shit. How in the hell did he find me?

I reached for the door handle, my hand slightly trembling. I shook it off. I had no reason to be nervous. Furious or not, he could kiss my ass. Finally, I turned the handle and opened the door.

"Well, this is a surprise … Cade," I said, my hand finding my hip.

"Spook," he corrected, moving his eyes behind me and flaring hotter.

I looked back to see Taylor had followed me. *Shit, shit, shit.*

I turned back toward the angry man. "Spook, what do you need?"

His eyes pinned me with intensity. "*You* were supposed to be at the clubhouse an hour and a fucking half ago. Instead, you're here with him." He stepped across the threshold, invading my space. "You like playing fucking games, Trixie?"

"Hey, hey, hey." Taylor pushed me behind him, which had Cade's eyes dropping to focus on where Taylor's hands were on me.

Oh, that was a stupid move.

"Get the fuck out of here," Taylor said as Cade's fury shifted to him.

Cade's eyes glided up and down Taylor, his face twisting into disgust. "Fucking pretty boy," he muttered. "Get the fuck out of here before I fuck your face up beyond repair."

Taylor's back stiffened, and I could only guess that he figured out who the man was at my doorstep, considering Cade was wearing his leather.

I stepped around Taylor. "Ca—whatever." *Why in the hell did he have to change his damn name?* This slip up was getting on my nerves. "I think you should go," I told him, only to have that anger come back to me, which made my insides shrink. Nevertheless, I wouldn't let it show. Instead, I stood strong and confident.

Cade shook his head. "Get him the fuck out of here now, Trixie." He balled his hands into fists, itching for a fight, something I did not want happening on my doorstep.

When I turned to Taylor, I could see he wanted an explanation, but I'd rather not. The night needed to be over. The sooner, the better for us all.

"I think you should go," I told Taylor.

"I'm not leaving you alone with *him*," he clipped as if Cade was beneath him, which rubbed me the wrong way. "He kills people," he added quietly.

"Yeah, motherfucker, I do. You wanna be next on that list?"

Taylor looked at Cade, something passing through his eyes, before he hastily grabbed his jacket.

"Screw this; you're not that great of a lay, anyway."

My mouth dropped open. "Get the fuck out of here," I growled at him, my veins pumping with anger. That had stung, considering I thought what we had was pretty damn good.

"Fine. If you wanna be with trailer trash, go for it."

It happened so fast, I swore if I blinked, I would have missed it. One moment Taylor was standing beside me, and the next Cade had him pressed to the door with his forearm against his throat.

Taylor grabbed at Cade's arm that rippled with muscles as he tensed, but he was unsuccessful.

"Talk like that again to her, and I'll fucking cut your dick off and stick it in your ass," Cade growled as my stomach dropped. That was just gross. "You open your mouth about Trixie, not just me, but me *and* my boys are coming for you. Our trailer trash will fucking destroy you, pretty boy." Cade gave him one more hard press to the throat then shoved him out the door.

Taylor lost his balance and fell to the ground, stumbling backward, away from Cade.

"Fuck," he groaned, holding his throat as he ran to his car.

That was the last I saw, because Cade closed the door, his angry attention now on me.

I took a few steps back, his eyes telling me that I needed to get away. Needed to run.

"Ca …" I shook my head, trying to get it on straight. "Spook, I think you should go."

He stalked toward me as my legs bumped into the back of the recliner. Then his body was pressed to mine, his face so damn close I could feel his forced breaths. Too close.

"Trixie, I didn't take you for a game player." His jaw ticked with his anger. "I told you last night I fucking *want* you. Apparently, you don't know what that means, so I'm gonna fucking show you."

He slammed his lips on mine, the kiss bruising, claiming, and owning me. He didn't just kiss me. No, he *took* me, not giving me a choice in the matter. All I could do was follow along with him.

Just like yesterday, he gave me no room to breathe, and I couldn't help myself; his lips were too damn perfect. This was all too consuming. Too much. I couldn't go there with him.

I brought my hands up to his hard chest, giving him a push as I tried tearing my lips from his. He didn't budge. Instead, he followed my movement, wrapping his arm around my waist, pulling me to his body firmly. With his other hand, he squeezed my breast, and I could do nothing except kiss him back.

This wasn't the same as Taylor. No, this was rough, hard, and so damn good it wiped all remnants of Taylor from my head. This was what I had been missing tonight.

He coaxed me with his lips, compelled me, challenged me, forced me to lose the battle. My body loved our connection, even though my mind knew I should fight harder, struggle more to get out of his embrace. Unfortunately, the adult version of Cade was so much better than the kid. As much as I would berate myself for doing this later, I couldn't stop now.

I whimpered into his mouth, the taste of tobacco and Cade dancing on my tongue. I clutched his hard shoulders where the leather was so soft, a contrast against his rough attack. My body sprang to life. I swore I could feel his brutal kiss through every nerve ending.

He moved his hands up my cami, pulling it off in a swift move and exposing my breasts. The cool air hit my nipples, making them hard as pebbles, or maybe that was him.

He lifted my leg until the crook of my knee rested on his hip, connecting my heat with his hard erection. Then he lifted me, and my legs wrapped around his hips as he carried my weight.

It was then that I turned my mind completely off as the pleasure from his touch took over, sending me to a place I hadn't been … ever.

I continued kissing him, our tongues fighting for control until he overpowered me. My heart rate raced through the roof. I ached horribly, needing release, one that I now knew only he could satisfy.

He carried me directly to my bedroom. It didn't even click until later that he knew exactly where it was.

Cade tossed me onto my bed, looking down at me, lust oozing from him.

"Shorts off," he ordered, and my brain started to kick in now that his lips weren't attacking me.

What in the hell are you doing, Trix?

"Spook, I can't do this with you," I told him without my known confidence, scurrying up the bed and trying to get some space between us. My mind raced too fast. I needed to think, and not having a shirt on didn't help.

"You're wrong, Trixie. Your body fucking wants this." He stripped off his leather, placing it on my dresser, and then reached around over his shoulder blade and pulled his shirt off.

My arousal spiked as I took in each ripple of his chest. Damn, the differences in his body hit me hard. Still lean but covered in tattoos and toned, he even had the defined abs I had only seen on television. Beyond sexy, and God, he was hot. So hot my body trembled with need.

"No, I don't. You need to go." Lies fell from my lips as my head fought a losing battle with my body.

He unbuckled the large, silver buckle on his belt and then unbuttoned his jeans, letting them fall to the ground in a heavy thump. His thick cock stood to attention, pointing straight up, the head an angry purple.

Gone was the boy I had last. What stood before me was all man. His deeply veined cock with its full mushroom tip called to be licked, and my mouth watered as my clit throbbed. The word horny didn't begin to describe how I was feeling.

He didn't acknowledge my words. "Shorts off," he repeated as my brain tried to justify my body's reactions.

Just treat this like another casual fuck with Taylor. A booty call.

Having sex with him meant nothing when I needed the orgasm. He came here. I shouldn't feel bad for this, for wanting him. It would be for old times' sake. Then I could rid him from my life for good.

And I'd already made my mind up about Nanette, so I wasn't doing this to get something from him. No, this would be for pure pleasure, just two people fucking. Besides, how many people went home with strangers from bars? Tons. This would be no different.

Realization hit me in my wound-up state that my justifications might have been warped, but at this point, the decision was made.

I pulled down my shorts, wiggling my hips to get them off, displaying my white thong. He moved to the edge of the bed, grabbing my foot and pulling me so I ended up flat on my back. With my skin against the soft fabric beneath me, I gave a sharp cry as he covered me with his hard body. His lips on mine, he fell between my thighs.

Fuck, this man could kiss.

I laced my fingers through his silky hair as I pulled him closer. Since I had obviously allowed us to get this far, it was time for me to go all in.

It was with that thought in mind I snapped. I couldn't get close enough.

He ripped his lips away, his mesmerizing eyes boring down into mine. "No fucking guy touches you, Trixie. No one but me." He came back down, his lips on mine before I could respond. Really, I didn't want to talk. I wanted him to fuck me. I needed to relieve this burn.

He roamed my breasts, down my ribcage, across my stomach. Each touch of his calloused fingertips sent goosebumps across my flesh. He scored me, branded me, the bumps all turning into fire.

He pulled back. "You wet for me, Trixie?" He rose only enough to tear my panties from my body, his fingers swiping over my pussy.

I groaned as my hips bucked, needing more.

He showed me his fingers soaked with my arousal. "Fucking dripping." He brought his fingers to his mouth, licking every drop of me off.

Fuck, that was hot. Never had a man done *that* in front of me before. Fuck if it didn't make my clit pulse harder than I'd ever imagined.

"Not now, because I need to be balls deep inside you, but soon, I'm gonna eat that pussy until you fucking scream my name."

Wetness flooded me as his crude words catapulted me higher.

"You'd like that, wouldn't you?"

I moaned at his question and then screamed, "Would you just fuck me already!" I needed … more. He had me so tightly wound I would explode if he didn't do something.

"Condom?" he asked, and I reached over to the nightstand, pulling one out of the drawer. He took it then rolled it over himself. He grabbed my knees and spread me wide as he looked down at my pussy.

I knew my pussy looked good, but with his careful inspection, a slight trepidation came over me. I tried to shut my legs, but he held them open.

"Fuck, your pussy is perfect: pink, plump, and throbbing. I can't wait to get my mouth on it."

I felt a blush creep up my neck to stain my cheeks. Never had a guy tell me that before, either.

His eyes locked on mine. "This won't be like before. I didn't know shit back then." He thrust into me in one deep stroke, and I squirmed, trying to make room for him inside my body as I cried out from the intrusion.

He stilled, waiting for me to accommodate him. After a few moments, I expanded, wrapping around him. He was big, bigger than I'd ever had inside me, bigger than he had been fifteen years ago. The stretch bordered on painful but still so damn good.

"Fuck, you're so goddamned tight." He began to thrust, dragging his dick in and out of my body. "Better than I fucking remembered."

He made computing those words difficult. I could only focus on the in and out strokes of his body in mine, heaven mixed with hell, wrapped together in something I'd never experienced before.

He held my knees firmly, opening me wide to him as he plunged into my body with such force the headboard knocked on the wall over and over again. Then, lost in sensation, it didn't register when he let my knees go.

The combination of him pinching my nipples and his movement inside of me spiked my arousal as my clit hummed. He rubbed my swollen nub hard, and I let go.

Arching my back, I let loose a scream that echoed throughout the room. My entire body quivered as shards of pleasure overtook me.

"Fuck me," he growled above my quaking body. It took me moments to open my eyes to meet Cade's. "You didn't fucking come like that the first time." His eyes narrowed. "I'd have fucking remembered that." He pressed his cock deep inside of me, stilling. It wasn't painful. No, the spot he hit revved me back up for another go.

"Cade," I gasped, digging my nails into the flesh of his tattooed arms.

He lifted my knees then pulled my legs together, bending them in front of me until the tops of my shins rested on his hard chest. He came down on me, pressing my knees to my breasts as his thrusts became more demanding. In and out, over and over. The sensations grew, this angle hitting the top wall of my pussy. Droplets of sweat beaded his brow from his exertion, falling to my chest.

"Fuck, you're so goddamned hot," he growled, his plunges reminding me of a steam engine going in rapid bursts.

Then it hit. Hard. Long. Life exploding. From the tips of my toes, up my legs, torso, arms, and head. I screamed my release, not caring if I woke up the neighborhood as I let the pleasure invade every molecule of my body. I felt as if I were floating on a cloud, zapped with a lightning bolt as my body convulsed. Nothing, absolutely nothing, mattered in that moment. I felt free for the very first time in my life.

I kept my eyes closed, enjoying the moment, not wanting it to end or for the euphoria to disappear.

Cade stilled above me. "Fucking hell," he ground out as he pressed hard inside me with his release, my pussy contracting around him as I felt his cock twitch with his orgasm.

He released his weight on me, his face sinking into my neck, his nose on the sweet spot between my ear and my shoulder. Flashes of our first time bombarded me as he took in several deep breaths.

Long minutes passed before he pulled out then rolled off to my side. I set my legs down, the stiffness from the angle making them tingle. Our labored breathing filtered in my bedroom, the smell of arousal and sex infiltrating my nostrils.

As I came back down from the frenzy, everything around me started to crash and burn. That wonderful feeling drifted away, and in its place were the consequences of my actions. The justifications I made earlier flew out the window in a swift whoosh.

I stared up at the ceiling, the last few moments hitting me hard. I had just fucked Cade Baker, something I told myself repeatedly I would not do again. Still, my dumbass did it, no questions asked.

I felt tears prick the backs of my eyes as the pain of losing him crashed over me, squeezing at my heart all over again. I steeled myself since last night, or I thought I had. Yet, here I lay, still feeling Cade between my legs.

What have I done?

Making matters worse, he gave me the best sex I'd ever had.

My heart thudded, trying to come back to life, while I tried with all my might to make it stop.

This was just a booty call, like another casual fuck with Taylor. Nothing more.

Nothing more.

FIVE

SPOOK

SHE LIED ALL THOSE YEARS AGO, telling me the sex had been great for her. It fucking wasn't. Not with the way she just looked when she exploded around me. She held nothing back, giving me everything, and I took more. Damn, it was the sexiest thing I'd ever seen. It hit me in more ways than expected, dredging up old feelings I kept locked inside. Ones I hadn't thought I'd ever feel again.

I sucked in a breath then rolled toward her, the condom still on. My cock still stood half-erect, even after I had just come so fucking hard.

She turned to me, looking more beautiful than when I saw her earlier, because now she had my whisker burns on her skin, my scratches and my reddened marks. Her eyes were wide, hair wild. The just fucked look was magnetic on her. Mine, not that fucker who had been here earlier.

I lost my shit, unable to believe she fucking had another man here. Trixie needed to realize this was not a one-time gig. The thought of her with another man made my blood boil with rage. That shit wasn't happening again.

"Bathroom?" I asked, needing to get the fucking condom off my dick.

She lifted her finger, pointing to a door on the far side of the room, no words coming out of her mouth.

I bent over, kissing the tip of her nose. "Be back."

I took care of business and came back to find my woman covered from neck to toe with a sheet. I smirked. The damn woman wasn't just sexy; she also had the cute thing down. She'd always had that. From the first moment I saw her, she grabbed me and still fucking did. It was the little things like this that made Trixie who she was.

"You can go now," she said, holding the sheet so securely her knuckles were white. It was like she wanted to hide from me. Her eyes were working hard, though. Something told me she was re-erecting the walls she had built between us, trying to fortify them. She'd shown me way too much, and now she wanted to take it all back.

I don't fucking think so. She gave me everything. No way in hell would I allow her to try to push me away. I had a fucking sledge hammer to knock down those walls.

I climbed onto the bed, blanketing her body with mine. Every inch of my heat touched hers even with the fabric between us. The thump of her heart beat against my chest in rapid succession. I fucking got to her. Damn straight I did, and I wouldn't let go.

"What are you doing?" she asked, her eyes wide, jaw slacked.

I bent down, brushing my nose against her jaw bone, then came back up to stare into her beautiful green eyes. "We're not done, Trixie. Not by a fucking long shot." I pressed my lips to hers, taking exactly what I wanted.

She stiffened then moved, trying to get away.

"You need to …" Her words were muffled by my mouth. Whatever she was about to say, I didn't want to hear it. I didn't give a shit.

I gripped her hair, deepening the kiss. She tried to resist but failed as she began to soften. Her hands fell from the sheet between us, her fingers threading through my hair. Damn, I fucking loved the slight pulls she gave without even realizing how they only made my cock harder for her.

So many fucking nights after that first taste I had of her, all I thought about was Trixie. I wanted to pinch my damn self to make sure it was real, but her lips told me the answer. Even after fifteen years, I never forgot that first fucking taste of her.

Trixie had been the only girl in my entire life that I actually dated for any period of time. She spun herself around me so fucking tight back then I didn't think I'd ever come up for air. It was happening again.

When she finally let me inside her that first time, I came to the stark realization of her virginity. I waged a war within myself. Should I? Shouldn't I? She was too sweet, too Trixie. I wanted that. I wanted to be her fucking first. I wanted her, so I took it. It was mine—always had been, always would be. Even fifteen years ago, I was still a selfish bastard.

Unfortunately, life sucked, and I couldn't keep her. My sick fuck of a father ruined it, and I had to call it off. I couldn't say the words, though, so I did the only other thing I could. I ignored her. It hurt like hell, but it was for her own good.

I remembered seeing her stares directed my way, her avoidance, the way she had taken another path at school so she wouldn't have to see me. And I felt like an ass, but that was what had to happen. I had a job to do for my club. As much as it killed me, I had to let her go.

I pulled away from her lips, loving when she raised her head to follow, only to fall back into the pillow. Her jade green eyes fluttered open as if she were lost. Fuck, her eyes were the sexiest ones I'd ever seen. With her pupils dilated, the color took my breath away.

I brushed the hair away from her cheek, pinning it behind her ear. Her head tilted as I did, almost shyly.

"I…"

I held my finger to her lips, quieting her instantly. I refused to hear any crap about me leaving. I wasn't fucking going anywhere except back inside her heat, staying in her bed and in her life.

"We'll talk later. We've got shit to discuss, but tonight, let me make up for fifteen years ago."

A low noise escaped her throat, her eyes turning as round as saucers. I could see them working, moving back and forth, no doubt what I did to her all those years ago plaguing her head.

She began to shake her head. "No, we have nothing …"

I pressed my finger harder against her mouth, making her words sound like incoherent mumbles. Regardless, I knew she was protesting because the starch in her spine came back.

"I get you, baby. We'll hash all of it out later."

She tilted her head to nip at my finger, but I quickly pulled it away from her teeth. The little minx.

"We are not doing this, Cade. Once, that was it. No more."

I watched her eyes widened at my smile. I felt devilish, so I could only imagine what I looked like.

"Once didn't even scratch the itch, Trixie."

"Don't care," she snapped back, beginning to move below me. I loved that she actually thought she could squirm away from me. "It scratched mine, so that's it. You need to go now."

Laughing probably wasn't the best thing to do with her glare turning menacing in a cute way, yet I couldn't help myself.

"We'll see about that." I crashed my lips to hers as I lifted my body just enough to remove the sheet. She tried to keep ahold of it, but I was able to rip it out of our way.

She didn't kiss me back, but no way would I give up that easily. I kept at it until her nails dug into my shoulders, and some of that sass melted away from her as she kissed me back.

I broke the kiss, moving to her jaw, down her neck, down her collarbone to her plump tits, making her tremble. Fuck, I was a tits man. Lucky for me, Trixie had ample ones. And they were the best because they were fucking real—none of that fake-ass shit with her.

I kissed between them, cupping each in a hand. I squeezed hard, kneading them, the flesh so damn soft. Her back arched, inviting more. Lucky for her, the mood struck me to give her more, a lot more.

I kissed up her breast, finding a pert, hardened, pink nipple. I sucked it deep inside my mouth, continuing my assault on the other.

The sounds that came from her were so damn sexy my cock twitched, wanting some attention. *In due time. Let's enjoy this shit.*

"God, why do you have such a great mouth?" she moaned.

"Better to eat you with." I kissed my way over to the other nipple, giving it the same attention.

Using the wetness from the other, I pinched then rolled the tight tip. Trixie's hips bucked as she pulled my hair hard, the pain exciting me more, driving my lips to allow the suction to take over. Her breathing turned ragged. It was my fucking goal to make her breathless.

I moved from breast to breast over and over again until her hips bucked so insistently that I had to give her a reprieve.

As I moved down her body, her skin felt like silk to my lips, each touch soft and inviting. I dove into her navel, executing circle after circle with my tongue. I could smell her from here, the scent of her pussy making my mouth water. I needed to fucking taste her, really devour her.

I kissed down her stomach, her muscles quivering as I moved. The small patch of dark hair trimmed to perfection covered her mound. I fucking loved that she took care of herself.

Rubbing my nose in her soft curls, I swiped her pussy with my finger, the wetness making it an easy glide.

"Cade!" She jerked her hips, attempting to get away or follow. I couldn't tell which, but I realized quickly that I might need to hold her ass down.

"Smells so fucking good, Trixie," I told her as she started to tremble.

"You should stop." The words came out as an achy moan, letting me know she didn't mean them for a second.

"Babe, your body doesn't lie." I nipped her before I moved farther down, pulling her legs apart revealing my next meal.

The lips of her pussy were plump with a darkish pink tint. The outer lips were perfect. Her hard clit popped out from under its hood, begging for my mouth.

I couldn't wait a second longer.

As I licked from ass to clit, her female, sweet musk exploded on my tongue. Fuck me. She was beyond sweet, more like candied, even honey, and so damn fucking good. I sucked on her outside lips before pushing my tongue into her body in quick succession.

I put my arm over her waist to hold her down as she tried bouncing her hips.

Then I grabbed her nub between my teeth, giving it a small bite as she screamed out. I sucked hard while diving my fingers into her tight pussy, moving from her inner to outer lips to her clit over and over again, feeling her writhe below me.

When I felt her close to climax, I pulled back, wanting her to come on my cock.

"Don't stop," she groaned.

I looked up, the sight steeling my dick. Her eyes were closed, head thrown back in passion, clutching the sheets with white knuckles. Fuck, it was beautiful.

I went back to licking, nipping, biting and sucking every part of her pussy, taking each drop of her into my mouth as she continuously grew wetter and wetter. Her body began to tremble with her need. She was more than ready for me.

With one more delicious swipe to her clit, I moved back up her body despite her moans of protest. I reached for a condom, slipping it on, then kissed her lips as she dug her nails hard into my back while wrapping her legs around my hips, trapping me in place. The woman was damn strong.

I ripped my mouth away. "You want my cock inside you again, Trixie? Want me to take you hard and rough? Pound into your body with every muscle in me until you scream my fucking name?"

She moaned. My words. I could tell she fucking loved the crudeness. Thank Christ, too, because I couldn't be anyone else but me.

"Want me to drag my cock in and out so hard all you hear is the slap of our flesh connecting over and over again?"

Her hips bucked. "Would you just fuck me already!"

I was pretty sure she wanted those words to come out angry, but she missed the mark on her delivery. They came out breathy and wanton. Damn, I needed to fucking be inside her.

I lifted my hips and drove inside her to the hilt. Her eyes widened as she screamed from the invasion. Her pussy clamped around my cock so hard it took everything I had to keep from blowing my load at that very moment like a fucking teenager.

"Can't go slow," I growled, not thinking I'd ever be able to go slow with Trixie. She flipped so many damn switches inside of me that my control was on a short leash.

"Do it." She arched into me, her tits pushing into my chest.

I let go, ruthlessly pushing in and out of her. Leaning down, I took one of her nipples in my mouth and bit it before sucking.

She dug her fingertips hard into my shoulders, so much so I wouldn't be surprised if she drew blood, and I didn't fucking care. I wanted her, every goddamned inch of her.

With my left hand, I rubbed hard over her clit, showing no mercy as her pussy tightened around my cock. She was ready to explode, and fuck, it felt good, so damn good.

As she came, I had to stop thrusting; her grip on me was like a damn vice. Her shudders wracked her body, and I swore not one inch of her didn't convulse.

When she finally let go of my cock and I was about ready to blow … an idea struck.

I pulled out, ripping off the condom and sat between her sprawled thighs, pumping my cock hard and fast. Come raced from me, splattering all over her stomach, her pussy, even up to her tits as she heaved in and out, trying to breathe.

Fucking knew I'd make her breathless. With my dick still in hand, I gave it a few more strokes, and Trixie's eyes were on every movement, only turning me on more.

"Like watching me pump my cock?"

She nodded and licked her lips. Fuck.

"My come's all over you. Fucking love it."

I released my cock and smeared my come into her skin, around her stomach, up her breasts, and down by her pussy. She did nothing but lay there, accepting every swipe.

"Fuck, that's so goddamned hot."

Trixie smiled, and it lit up the whole goddamned room. Fuck, she was beautiful.

"I'm all sticky now."

"Best fucking look I've ever seen on a woman," I growled, looking down at her.

She was utter perfection. She'd grown so much since that first time I had her. Her curves were ones a man like me could hold on to and fuck hard without worrying I'd break her in half. Her legs were toned, but they had enough meat to wrap around my hips nicely. The dip between her hip and stomach made my mouth water. Fuck, I was getting hard again. This fucking woman turned me inside out.

She blushed, which was pretty fucking cute. Beneath the attitude, she was all softness. Fucking loved that.

Had to be hard in my life, but when I wanted sweet, I needed that too. What was even better, I had every indication her reaction was more to my words than her body. She owned her figure, enjoyed it, reveled in it. She wasn't covering herself up, trying to hide. No, her hiding came from somewhere else. I sensed there were emotional wounds she didn't want me to see.

"I need to go clean up," she said, her eyes still not coming down from the high I'd just given her. If she left this bed, though, it would come crashing down, and she'd let her brain start putting those fucking walls back up again.

I lay back down on top of her, my sticky release between the two of us. Fuck, even that was hot. I rolled to my side, pulling her to my body as closely as I could.

"Later," I murmured, kissing her lips softly.

"I'm all gross, and now you're all gross. I'm not staying like this," she fired back, her spark igniting.

I smiled at the little fireball. "It's unbelievably hot." I pressed my semi hard cock against her thigh.

"You're ready to go again already?" she asked incredulously, and I laughed.

"Not quite yet. Give me a bit. You've already milked me dry twice. Need a little recoup time."

She relaxed a bit in my arms, but her eyes didn't meet mine.

"Are you clean?" she asked.

"Guess we should have talked about that," I mused. "Yeah, I'm clean. Get checked routinely, but I'll have our guy run the tests to make sure. You on the pill?"

She stilled. "It doesn't matter, because this is over."

"Answer the fucking question," I retorted, squeezing her just a bit.

"I am, but it doesn't matter, because like I said, this is the last time."

I said nothing, just settled in, holding her. She wanted a fight, and I wasn't going to give it to her.

"You wanna talk now or sleep?" I asked after long moments passed in silence.

"I'm not sleeping covered in your sticky mess. And you're not staying here," she protested, meeting me straight on.

I fucking loved that shit. Loved how she didn't back down.

"So, let's talk, then."

"I don't think that's a good idea, either," she retorted, her lip giving the slightest curl before she wiped it away.

"I could just fuck you again."

She rolled her eyes and countered, "How about a shower?"

That sounded like a fucking excellent plan.

"Now you're talkin'." I rolled from the bed, and she followed, looking down at my seed spread across her.

I fucking loved leaving my mark on her. Never wanted to mark a woman before, but with Trixie, I'd wanted to mark her since I saw her in the hallway when we were kids, put my permanent stamp on her.

I stepped to the side as she walked past me, her ass shaking with each step. I slapped it, and she turned around and yelped.

"Why did you do that?" she asked quickly.

"Had to. Sexy ass in front of me, had to slap it."

She gave me a roll of the eyes then turned on the water, feeling it before stepping in.

I took a quick piss then joined her. The hot spray of the water fell over her body as she lathered up her hands and began to scrub off everything I had just put on her.

I pulled her hands away.

"What?" she asked.

"Let me." I grabbed the soap, lathered it, and started at her neck.

I made slow circles with my thumbs, feeling her throat bob from swallowing deeply. I moved to her shoulders, breasts, down her front, and then landed on my knees in front of her as she stood stock-still. Then I rose and turned her around to rinse off her body.

I gave the same attention to her back, making sure to cup her ass roughly. Fuck, her body was amazing, and I enjoyed every second of touching it.

"What are you doing?" she whispered.

I placed my lips to her ear. "Cleaning you."

"I get that, Cade, but why?" Her voice came out a bit timid, unsure.

I turned her. "Because I like doing it." I took her lips again and pressed her body to mine. I stole her breath with a kiss, taking it for my own. "Fucking enjoy it."

I looked for the shampoo, noting strawberries on the label. Grinning to myself, I realized then the reason I always smelled the sweetness on her.

I turned Trixie toward the water. "Tip your head back."

She eyed me wearily. The trust wasn't there. I knew I had broken it long ago, but it was time to start building it back up.

"I can do it myself," she protested.

"Trixie …" I warned.

It must have clicked in her head that I meant business, because she slowly turned toward the spray.

"Tip your head," I reminded her when she paused a bit too long for my liking.

A slow motion reel took place, or at least, if felt that way since it took her so long to comply. I'd just been inside this woman, and it hurt that she didn't trust me enough to wash her hair. I had my work cut out for me.

As she wet her hair, I enjoyed watching the water cascade down her body. When she finally tilted her head forward again, I squirted shampoo in my hands then massaged it into her head.

"I don't get this. It feels too …" She trailed off, a moan escaping her as my fingers dug into her scalp.

"Good?" I finished.

"Oh, yes," she said almost blissfully.

I pulled her back gently into the water. Rinsing the soap from her sexy hair, I then massaged again with the conditioner.

This time, I gave attention to her neck. I felt each knot she was carrying around with her, attempting to knead each one out.

The water started to cool, so I put her head under again, getting all the conditioner out before it got frigid.

"Thanks," she whispered softly, moving to the side so I could quickly wash my body.

"You done?" I asked.

At her nod, I turned off the faucets, reached out, and grabbed a towel. I toweled her off first then wrapped it around her body before grabbing one for myself, doing the same.

When I followed her into the bedroom, she turned around abruptly, and I ran smack into her.

"Cade, I really think you should go now," she said firmly, her eyes soft yet worried.

"Get in bed. Let's sleep, and we'll deal with all this shit tomorrow." I pushed her lightly to the bed, tearing the towel from her body.

"Hey!" she exclaimed. "I was drying off!"

I smiled. "Bed. Sleep."

She glared at me, hands on her hips. It took everything I had to hold back a chuckle.

"You're awfully bossy." She may have thought that, but she climbed into the bed, anyway.

"Babe, you have no idea yet." I lay down beside her and gathered her into my arms.

She attempted to pull away. "You might be bulldozing your way into my bed, but I am not cuddling with you."

"I'm holding you," I declared as I pulled her back to my front again.

Her body was tense. I knew she thought she wanted space from me, but I couldn't give her that. No more space. However, I could compromise and let her face away from me if it was what she needed.

It took a long time for her to relax and fall asleep. Then, a long while later, deep in sleep, Trixie rolled over toward me as I was still replaying the night's events. Her arm crept across my chest, and she tucked her head under my own, a small sigh leaving her lips.

Fuck, this was how it was supposed to be all those years ago.

She had no clue yet, but I wasn't letting this shit go. Still, I knew *my* Trixie would be a challenge, though a challenge I would win.

I woke to a very cold bed. My hand reached out, touching nothing. I listened, but I didn't hear a sound. It surprised me. I usually slept lightly, never knowing when I needed to be on guard. Something about being in bed with her, having her cuddled up to me, had me sleeping like a fucking log.

Rolling out of bed, I grabbed my pants and shirt, throwing them on along with my cut, socks, and boots. I walked down the hall of the little ranch house.

"Trixie?" I called into the nothingness.

I looked through the house, but she was nowhere. The little minx jumped out on me.

A piece of paper on the table had a large scrawl on it.

Spook,

I had shit to do. Lock the bottom lock when you leave. Please don't come back.

I chuckled. Woman had no fucking clue who she was dealing with. Oh, I'd be back … tonight or this afternoon. I hadn't decided yet.

"Fucking hell." I tossed the papers down to the desk.

Nothing was going right today. One of the guys scratched a custom paint job on a tank, costing me a shit load to redo it. The phone rang off the hook, but I passed that shit off to Stiff. I needed to let go of some of this work and pass it to the other guys, but even after all this time, the mess my father had made had me leery to relinquish control. Although I didn't have many fears in life, seeing my club go back down the shitter was one of them. That was why I worked my ass off every damn day: to make certain it didn't happen. However, it was starting to wear on me. There had to be a better way. I just needed to find it. I needed more help.

It wasn't that I didn't trust my brothers. I didn't trust life.

"What's going on, boss?" Boner asked, coming into the office.

"Too much shit and not enough hands," I told him, running my fingers through my hair.

He took a seat in front of my desk. "It's about time you delegate," he said calmly, pulling out a smoke and lighting it. I grabbed mine and did the same. "Gotta let go of this shit."

I rubbed my hand over my face. "I know, man. Let's start figuring out who can do what. Then we'll bring it to the table."

He nodded. "How was your piece last night?"

My blood lit at the mention of my *piece*. Trixie was anything but.

"Don't bullshit me," I growled. "You of all people know the history, so don't play fucking stupid. She's fucking *mine*, and I'll do whatever I have to in order to get her back."

He held up his hands, his palms facing me. "Still hot for her after all these years, bro?"

I said nothing, and he whistled.

"Damn, Spook's ready to turn in his house mouses."

After being inside Trixie, no house mouse could hold a fucking candle to her.

I was fucked, but for the first time, it was a fucked I liked.

SIX

TRIX

"**Y**OU GET ANYWHERE WITH CADE?" Jett asked as she plopped down in the chair in front of my desk. She had a beauty that pulled everyone in and curves that made me insanely jealous. Her long, dark hair laid pencil straight, and her eyes were a blue that looked almost gray in different lights.

My stomach fell at her question, reminding me of last night. I couldn't believe I fucking slept with him. Not just fucked him, but showered with him, fell asleep with him … woke up in his damn arms. *Sneaky bastard.*

I could still feel him between my legs. Hell, I even had phantom feelings of him inside of me. He'd had a lot of practice. I knew he had because I had heard all about it. And I wasn't any better than one of those paid hookers.

Fucking moron. My reasons had sucked before. They meant shit now.

I wanted to pass off the night as being just another booty call, a way to fuck each other out of our systems, but both were a flat out lie. Last night was so much more than anything Taylor, or any of my other weak-ass booty calls, and I had ever been.

The rawness in his eyes captivated me. God, his eyes … I could see so much more in them last night. More than I'd ever thought I would see. But I was just fooling myself. I wouldn't go back fifteen years to fall for the bad boy again, just to get my heart smashed all over again.

Mortification didn't even cut it when it came to describing how I felt. Weak. Pathetic. I gave in, letting him have that power over me with his smooth talking and fantastic bed skills. Plus, he had looked sexy as hell in his leather and jeans. To see him on a motorcycle, too, was just a recipe for disaster. And I had just spread my legs, begging for him to give it to me. *Dammit.*

Although I was dead serious in the note I left him this morning, it felt really odd to leave it for him in my own house. Nevertheless, I couldn't stay and deal with the morning after shit. One look and I would have let him inside my body again. I would have let him take me over and over until I really couldn't walk. Now that I knew how much he had grown, let alone changed in the bedroom, it would be more difficult than ever to say no to him.

I had to remember Cade crushed me. My first love left me to pick up the pieces of my torn heart. I couldn't go back to the me from that time.

"He doesn't know if Nanette is there." I decided to leave out the whole him fucking my brains out bit. I wouldn't open up that can of worms. I told Jett all about Cade one night after way too many shots of tequila. Regardless, the less people who knew about the now, the better.

Her brow rose. "Is he gonna look? Surely, the clubhouse isn't that big."

No. He could have looked while I was there a couple of nights ago, but no. Why would he make this easy? That would be ludicrous.

"The bottom line is, I'm gonna have Ike on her. The chances of me getting my money back are slim, but I won't stop until I find her. I knew better. I'm taking it as another lesson learned. Now I deal." I grabbed a pen on the desk and placed the cap between my teeth. Old habits were hard to break. Chewing on pen caps seemed to relieve some of my tension. The crunch of the plastic between my teeth always helped me focus.

"What about the girls?" she asked, concern blazing in her eyes.

I bit down harder. "I'll deal with that if it comes up. I'm not gonna worry about it, because it might not even be an issue. If, by chance, it is, I'll take care of it then."

Because Hell would freeze over before I went to Cade for anything else.

She shrugged, calmness coming back into her features. "Your problem, boss lady." She shook a manila folder she held in her hand. "Gotta go over these."

For the next two hours, we went through numbers.

I kept everything on point with my business. My father didn't have a loving hand. Instead, he taught me the hard way through lots of tests. Some, I passed; most, I failed. I never knew when an assessment would start or end. Therefore, I treated everything like one. That way, I did my best no matter what. The sad thing was, almost everything he did was to evaluate me and see my worth, which hadn't been much to him.

I leaned back in my chair, relieved. "Thank God that's done." I tossed the chewed up pen onto the desk.

Jett's lip curled with disgust. "Gross, throw that away."

I rolled my eyes and tossed it into the trash.

A loud thump came from the other side of the door. Then a "you motherfucker" was heard, followed by another loud crash, the sound of flesh meeting flesh, a man's heaves and gasps for air …

Jett looked at me, her eyes filled with concern. I grabbed my 9mm from under my desk, clicking off the safety.

"Over here," I whispered to Jett.

She did as told, getting behind me, while I held the gun up to the door as more thumps and groans could be heard. Then the knob to the door began to turn.

"Stop right fucking there!" I yelled as the door flew open without pause, my finger on the trigger. I aimed at Cade who looked as calm as could be with the end of my barrel on him. "What in the sam hell are you doing!" I screeched.

"Put the fucking gun down, Trixie." His deep voice echoed throughout my office.

Behind him, I saw Ike laid out on the floor.

"What the hell?" I slipped on the safety then put the gun behind my back before pushing past Cade. I knelt on the floor, seeing Ike had cuts with black and blue marks beginning to form. "Are you out of your fucking mind?" I questioned Cade from the floor.

He shrugged. "Fucker wouldn't let me back here."

I was a bit astonished that he didn't even have sweat on his brow because the beating he dished out to Ike had to have taken some serious effort.

"I wanted back here. End of story."

"So you beat the shit out of him? You couldn't have just called?" As soon as the words left my mouth, I wanted to smack myself. I knew he'd snap at me about it.

"I could've, but I'm sure you wouldn't have answered."

I shook my head, turning my attention back to Ike. "Are you alight?"

He gave a muffled groan.

"Shit. Jett, call our guy. See if he can come and take a look."

Jett pushed past Cade. "Who's that?" she asked within ear shot of me.

"That asshole is Cade. Oh, wait, sorry, *Spook*." Her eyes widened as I felt Cade's presence above me. He grabbed my arm, lifting me from the floor. "Hey!"

"Deal with that," he ordered Jett then shut the door behind him as he released me.

"What the fuck do you think you're doing?" I barked, really thinking of grabbing my gun and shooting him in the damn leg for being an ass.

"You ran," he said as calmly as could be, yet his eyes were blazing mad. He didn't like me leaving him. Well, too damn bad.

I fed off the anger filling my veins. "I did not. I had work. Anyway, it was one night, Spook. That's it. One booty call to scratch an itch." Even as I said the words, my pussy clenched from remembering Cade inside of me, wringing orgasm after orgasm out of my body.

He stepped forward. I stepped back. The air in the room electrified as it bounced all around us, causing the hair on the back of my neck to rise in excitement.

My ass hit the desk, halting me, but he didn't stop until his face aligned with mine, his tobacco exhales caressing my skin. Fuck, I loved his smell.

"Trixie," he whispered so softly it caught me off guard, and my eyes flew to his. "Let's get a few things straight." His tone changed, becoming harsher. I didn't care for it much. "First, you do not leave a bed we are sleeping in and sneak the fuck out."

My mouth got the better of me. "Don't worry; it won't happen again."

He leaned back, a devilish smile crossing his utterly handsome face. "Wildcat, if I touch between your legs, you gonna be wet for me?"

I involuntarily closed my legs, not wanting him to feel, because he was fucking right. He didn't need to be told that, though.

"Yep, hot, wet, and ripe for me." His hips pressed against mine, the ridge of his steel cock demonstrating his arousal. Damn, I loved that he had that reaction to me. "Enough talking." His lips crashed onto mine, and my stupid body gave in wholeheartedly. *Again.*

He tilted his head, and I threaded my fingers through his hair. God, I loved the feel of his hair, so damn soft.

A loud crash came from behind me. I pulled away to see all the contents of my desk spread across the floor.

"You're cleaning that shit up," I told him.

He chuckled. "We'll see about that."

"I'm serious." I looked over at the huge-ass mess. "You're ..." I tried to argue, but his lips came down on mine again in a punishing kiss that sent me into a fog.

He pulled away. "Only way to shut you up is to kiss you or fuck you."

I opened my mouth to retort, but again, he covered my mouth with his while using his hands to roam over my body with urgency.

Wetness coated my panties as I did exactly what he said—I shut up, giving in.

He didn't tell me to strip this time. No, he knelt down in front of me and undid my pants, pulling them from my body. The gun clattered to the floor. The dumbass I was, I let him because each touch of his hands on my legs as he went only amped up my arousal for this man. How could one man turn me on this much?

"Hard and fast. I'm taking what I missed this morning."

I gasped as he turned me around, pressing my chest to the desk. I yelped as a slap came to my left ass cheek.

"You fucking hit me!" I growled, feeling the burn of the blow grow and settle in the V of my legs.

Thwack. Thwack. Two more blows.

I tried to move, but he held me with his arm across my back. I could have kicked, but the heat coming from his smacks felt so good.

"And you have five more coming. You leave the fucking bed again like that, this shit is doubled. Do it again, and I'm getting the fucking belt."

I began to protest just as three consecutive slaps came, only giving a slight pause before two more.

My entire backside burned, and my pussy throbbed and ached. I wanted to come—no, strike that. I *needed* to come.

Fuck. My brain turned into a pile of mush.

While I knew I should be yelling at him for hitting me, that I should be furious, my head floated to a place where nothing mattered, except the feelings in my body.

A pounding came on the door. "Trix, you okay?" Jett called out, obviously hearing us.

My mind semi-kicked in. "Yeah, take care of Ike," I yelled back, half-dazed.

"Okay."

I closed my eyes, letting the groans purr in my throat, as his heat blanketed me. His jeans rubbing over my burning ass made me jolt.

"Do. Not. Leave. The. Bed." He said each word so damn fiercely a shudder rippled through my chest. "You. Do. Not. Have another guy over to your house and give him *my* pussy." My brain ignited with that one.

I started to squirm, liking the happy place much better than this ... whatever it was.

"I'm not yours," I told him, trying to wiggle away, but his weight overpowered me.

"That's where you're wrong, Trixie. You've been mine for a long fucking time, and it's about time we right a wrong."

His words made no sense to me. He was the one who had disappeared from my life, not me. I was so damn infatuated with him I gave him the one thing I could never get back. And I wasn't talking about my virginity. No, my heart. He would never get that again, just so he could turn it to dust. No freaking way.

"You're talking out of your ass. Let me up," I demanded then kicked, barely missing his leg.

"Fucking kick me, and I'm tying your ass to the desk." He shook me gently. "Don't think I fucking won't."

I settled. The last thing I wanted was to be tied to the damn desk and have Jett or another employee come in. Fuck that.

"What is it you want, Spook?"

"It's Cade to you."

I shook my head. "You haven't even told me how you got your name."

"We have a lot of shit to talk about. My road name isn't one of them right now." He leaned toward my ear, his nose barely touching the outer shell, sending goosebumps down my neck, and answered my previous question. "You. All I fucking want is you."

My heart stopped. I couldn't speak. No sounds. Nothing would come from my lips. He had shocked me into utter silence. But then I shook my head.

Sex. He wanted sex. That was all he wanted. All he had ever wanted.

"You got your fill, so just leave me alone." My confidence came out in my words, filling me with pride.

He *tsked*. "Fill? No, wildcat, I have had nowhere fucking near my fill."

My heart did a little flip, and I wanted to scream at it to stop it. Sex. That's it. As long as I remembered that, I'd be fine. I went with just sex with Taylor for months. I could do it with Cade and not let my heart get involved. I could, but the question was, did I want to risk it? After last night's feelings started to pull from me, no, I didn't. The hurt before was too much. If I stayed on this path, it would be worse.

"Too bad. Your fill is officially over." All at once, I grabbed his arm, bucked my ass, and moved with a speed I didn't know I possessed. Then I darted across the room, out of Cade's reach. "Now you can go." I pulled down my shirt, knowing my thong was hanging out there, but fuck it. I owned that shit, running my fingers through my hair as if he hadn't just ripped my pants off.

"Games, games, games." He whistled deeply. "Told you I don't play fucking games."

"This isn't a damn game, Cade. This is my fucking life. I came to you to get one of my workers, not fuck you. This is my business, and you just beat the shit out of my guard. Enough is enough."

He shrugged, leaning a hip on the desk, his erection begging to come out of its confines. "I get that you don't know me now. We'll work on that. But know this: I don't fuck up an opportunity, and you coming to my clubhouse was exactly that."

"It was a mistake. You go on with your life; I go on with mine. Done." I brushed my hands back and forth as if to wipe myself clean of him.

He moved from the desk, stalking toward me.

"Oh, no, stay over there," I warned, but he didn't listen. I moved, and he moved in sync.

"If your ass would have been in bed this morning, we could have talked shit out. But you got scared and hightailed it out. I get that. I fucked up when we were kids. That's the thing, though, Trixie: we were kids." I stilled as he came toward me. "We need to talk about shit, and I can't do that when you run from me."

I crossed my arms over my chest. "Fine. Talk."

He shook his head. "Not like this. You're pissed; I'm pissed. We'll say shit and fuck all this up before we get a foot in the door. Now, I'm gonna bend you over that desk and fuck you until you can't walk. Then I'm leaving, and you're coming to the clubhouse tonight at seven."

I glared at him.

"If you don't want your ass smacked, I suggest you be there."

Damn, the thrill hit me again. I didn't even know I liked being spanked. I hated it as a kid. All of a sudden, it got me hotter than hell.

I went to sidestep him, but he ended up boxing me in. His lips came close to mine, and he whispered, "I know you want me to fuck you."

I shook my head, but my accelerated breathing told him otherwise. I knew it. He knew it. But my stubborn streak took over.

"No, I don't," I argued.

He touched my mound, and the air rushed from my body. All the need and want from before came back with a vengeance, curling and coiling around me like a snake, strangling me for release.

"I believe this. Your pussy tells me the truth."

"No—"

He cut me off with a searing kiss. I couldn't stop him. The kiss sucked all the fight out of me.

"Seems fucking you is the only way to shut that mouth of yours," he said as he pulled away.

"You—" My anger blared red hot, but once again, his kiss and my pathetic shoves—which, let's be honest, weren't the best—had me falling into his body. *Damn traitor.*

He led me back to my desk, and a rustle of paper filtered through the room. Then he flipped me over to my stomach, pushed my thong over my ass, and filled me to bursting.

I took everything he had to give. Everything.

I clawed at the wood, leaving indentations, and still, the desk moved across the floor with each powerful thrust, making a squeaking sound before he lifted my knee, putting it on top of the hard surface and giving him an even better angle.

"Fuck, your pussy is so damn tight," he groaned.

He circled the puckered rim of my ass with a finger, and I blew into cosmic space. Lights flickered behind my eyelids, dancing around, my body absorbing shock after shock after shock.

I heard Cade grunt then still above me, but I was wrung out. I couldn't move, couldn't think, couldn't do anything but be. My head felt as if I had been on a tilt-a-whirl.

His weighted heat pressed against me, but I didn't give a shit. I liked it. Then he went to my neck, to that special spot, breathing me in, and damn, I loved when he did that.

He brushed his hand from my upper chest down to my hip, bringing me back to the present, but a lot more slowly than I would have liked. In that touch, though, my brain kicked into gear.

I had done it again, even stayed still for him. He didn't have to hold me down or tie me up. Nope. I let him take more from me. Fuck, I was a damn idiot.

"Get off," I told him, trying to use my hands to push up off the desk, my breasts smashed to capacity.

He mumbled yet didn't move.

"Dammit, Cade, get the fuck off," I growled, angry with him but more pissed at myself.

He groaned and pulled out of me, falling into my office chair, while I hustled to my attached bathroom and locked the door. I sat on the toilet, my head in my hands, positive I had to be demented or one of those masochists wanting to hurt myself. That was the only reason I could come up with for giving in to Cade like this again.

It wasn't a dumbass booty call with him. It couldn't be. Too much heart was in the mix for it.

I may not know the man Cade was now, but from what I'd seen in the last two days, he wasn't going to give up. He chased off Taylor, threatened to beat the shit out of him, and then beat the hell out of my guard to get to me. I'd seen the determination in his eyes. And as much as I hated it, it turned me on.

I sat there, not knowing what in the hell I should do. I knew one thing, though. I would not be a coward. I would deal with Cade head on. Whatever he threw at me, I would handle it. I was a strong enough woman to do so.

I cleaned up, my hand on my pussy. Shit, did he use a condom? If he didn't, I'd fucking castrate him. I didn't feel anything dripping from me, but I had no clue when he would have put one on.

I walked hastily out the door, ready to ask Cade. I stood in shock, looking at the completely empty room, the contents of my desk still scattered to the floor. He had fucking left. Shit. Well, it served me right.

I looked at the garbage can where a condom tied at the end lay on top. *Thank God.*

I grabbed my clothes, threw them on, and went to check on Ike.

SEVEN

SPOOK

"*H*IT ME," I SAID INTO THE PHONE. On the other line, Lee was giving me the update I had been waiting for.

"She's pulling out of her drive and turning our way. I'm following."

Smart woman. Then again, I didn't think she'd attempt a no-show tonight, not after I dashed from her office. I knew it would piss her off. It was a contradiction to what I'd told her, but fuck it.

"Stay on her. Any detours, you call me. If not, I'll see you here in a few." I swiped the phone, turning it off as Boner came up, two beers in hand.

He handed me one, and I pulled off the cap before taking a healthy gulp. We weren't having a party, but we were hanging out, which always turned into something.

"What's goin' on, man?" he asked as we moved to the chairs off to the side, taking a seat. My view lined up with the parking lot, so I wouldn't miss Trixie when she pulled in.

"Waiting for Trixie," I answered, lighting a smoke.

He whistled before taking a pull off his beer. "You really sure you wanna open that up?"

"I'm tellin' her. No one else says shit."

He turned his head, his eyes blazing into mine, taking me in. "You're shitting me. You think she doesn't already know?"

I shook my head. "Nope. I honestly don't, and really, I don't have a choice. Tell the guys no one says a word to her."

If I made a go with Trixie, I needed to come clean. Unfortunately, my father's filth would still cling to me and now Trixie. I couldn't wash it off either of us.

Boner waited a beat then asked, "You do this, is there gonna be blowback?"

There might be. I didn't really know the answer to that. Regardless, I'd do everything in my power for there not to be.

"After we talk, I'll do what I can to make sure everything's smooth. Trixie isn't stupid; she'll know what to do with the information." *Lock it the fuck down.*

Trixie's car pulled into the lot, Lee behind her on his bike.

"Sure you wanna open all this shit up for pussy?"

I didn't think. One second, I was sitting, and the next, Boner had my hand around his throat.

His eyes blazed back into mine, shock and anger spearing me. I rarely exerted my authority around here since everyone knew where I stood, but Boner pushed me too far with this.

"Don't fucking say that shit again. Got me?"

His hands came to mine as I released him. "Fuck, brother."

I shook my head. "Not her, Boner. Fucking hear me now. Don't give me shit. Spread that."

He coughed. "Then answer me this. After you took your father out, why in the fuck didn't you go and get her back? If you wanted her so fucking badly, why now?"

I fucking hated when Boner got like this.

I grabbed my bottle, seeing Trixie's taillights go off, and took a pull from my beer. *Alright, shit.* "Because I know she's better off without me. I know she'll find out shit she doesn't need to know that exists in this fucking world, but now, none of that matters. Second chances don't just fall into your lap, Boner. Her coming back wasn't by fucking chance. I'm taking it and running. Consequences be damned."

I left Boner there, letting the word consequences roll through my head. Yeah, I'd had my fair share of those with Trixie. I needed to get through them then move the fuck on.

I tossed my smoke as Trixie opened the car door, her flat shoes hitting the blacktop. Then I saw torn jeans covering her sexy as hell legs. When she rose, I saw an emerald green top wrapped around her so fucking tight it gave me a great view of her tits. And then I noticed her long hair falling down to her waist in waves.

Fuck, she was beautiful. Thought that fifteen years ago, but now, fuck ... She was beyond anything I could have imagined.

The glower on her face didn't deter her beauty. Nope, it made me harder, even as she slammed her car door, shaking the vehicle.

"I don't need to be fucking babysat." She pointed to Lee getting off his bike. "That little shit followed me from my house. You think I couldn't find my way on my own?"

I didn't answer. Fuck no, not with her so close.

I yanked her body to mine, and her hands came to my chest. "What are you ...?"

I cut her words off, my lips attacking hers. Fuck, she tasted just like her strawberry shampoo mixed with her enticing smell. My dick ached, jumping behind my jeans.

It only took moments before she melted into me like ice cream. As the attitude disappeared with the kiss, I pulled back.

"I needed to make sure you came."

Her eyes snapped up, the attitude coming back in full-force. "And what? You think it's okay to have one of your ... club guys come and follow me?"

"First, they're my brothers. Second, fuck yeah. I'll give you a little time to realize how things work here, but babe, you're far from stupid. That's what tonight is: showing you my world."

"And you think showing me your *world*," she mocked, putting her hands in quotes around the phrase, "is gonna change my mind?" She shook her head, her attitude leaving and a bit of somberness settling in her eyes. "I get it. You wanna fuck me out of your system. I get it Ca—Spook, I do, but letting me meet your brothers and showing me your world isn't necessary for that. Having me here at your club isn't necessary. I told you I don't need your help with Nanette. I'm letting it ride."

I didn't believe that last part. No way was she the type of person to let that disrespect get past her. She was up to something.

She squeezed my arms, pulling me out of thinking about her words.

"Looks like we have more to talk about than I thought." I kissed her again, unable to be this close to her lips and not. "I'm not fucking you out of my system. Never fucking said those words to you."

"You did say you hadn't had your fill," she snapped.

"No, I said I hadn't had my fill *yet*." I pulled her securely to me. "Yet could be thirty years from now. Never fucking know what tomorrow will bring."

She gasped, as if the concept was out of left field.

"Just live in the fucking moment, Trixie. Live in the now. You're here, so let's see what the night brings us because you're not fucking leaving."

She yanked back. "Says who?"

"Babe, you really think I won't have a guy let the air out of your tires for the night?"

Her beautiful face lit up in anger. I fucking loved it. "Don't you dare," she warned.

I smiled, which only made her face twist more.

"I would dare. You're here with me for the fucking night."

"You want me to spend the night here …? At your club?"

A piece of hair blew across her cheek from the wind. I pulled it away, tucking it behind her ear. Loved the softness of her hair. She didn't use a gallon of hair products, making her hair stiff as hell. No, she was natural. Perfect.

"Yeah. Like I said, let's see what the night brings."

I kissed her, but this time, I slowed it down. I was a bastard for knowing exactly what to do to get her to soften up. I used it to my advantage whenever I could.

On one hand, my body was urging me to take, take, take. I needed to change things up, though. She wasn't going anywhere, and I needed her to see that, understand that. If she needed a little sweet with her ride, I'd give it to her. Then I'd give her rough and hard.

I released her, and she gasped like she hadn't breathed the entire time my lips were on hers. Then she tried to pull away, but I grabbed her hand and started walking toward the people in the back lounge area, tugging her along with me.

"You don't need to pull me along."

I tugged her hard then stopped, pulling her into my arms. "Fucking go with it, wildcat."

She rolled her eyes.

I should have put her over my knee and spanked that sexy as hell ass, but the more the fire came out of her, the harder my dick pressed against my jeans.

Her eyes dilated, and her breathing picked up. Then I brushed my lips against hers so damn gently I barely felt them. Her eyes widened. I chuckled.

"Sweet to go along with your sassy."

Her eyes turned into slits. Before she opened her mouth, though, I pulled her into the fray of people.

Boner stood in a wide stance, a beer in hand and his eyes on Trixie. "Well, well, well, if it isn't little Trixie Lamasters."

Trix stiffened as I wrapped my arm around her. "And you are?" she asked, her eyebrow rising.

"I remember you at your locker. My brother here watched you like a fucking hawk."

Alright, enough of that shit.

"Boner," I said in a low warning. "Knock it the fuck off."

Trixie didn't give two shits about the thickness between us. "Name," she said.

"Ben," Boner told her. "But no one calls me that, and you don't, either."

Her inhalation of breath told me she remembered him. I had no clue what ran through her head, so I kept quiet until she spoke.

"Well, shit. I'd have never guessed it was you." She shook her head. "You look …"

I chuckled.

"What the fuck are you laughing about?" Boner asked me, but I just shook my head.

"It's just … You grew up nice."

To that, I turned my attention to Trixie who had a wide smile on her face. Oh, fuck no.

Boner stepped closer, and my head whipped his way.

"You want me to hurt you?"

Boner laughed. "Nah, boss. Trixie, you sure grew up."

"So I've been told. You stuck around with this guy, huh?" She pointed at me. "Would have thought you were smarter than that."

Boner laughed harder. "Damn, Trixie, I don't remember you having so much sass or spunk." Boner rubbed his chin thoughtfully. "It's … nice."

That was what tonight was about. I wanted to make damn sure she could hold her own in my world, not that it would change the outcome. Getting her to listen would be a whole other job. First things first.

That business aside, I stepped up to Boner, eye to eye, breaking the contact between him and Trixie. Anger began to pulse through my veins like a drug. He was my brother, but he had been fucking warned several times. If he didn't quit, I'd make sure his nose bled.

"Stop."

Boner's lips quirked. "I get it, boss. If she's gonna be around us, she needs to get used to it. *You* need to get used to it."

Fuck, he had me there. Fucking hell.

I shook my head. I knew better, but it didn't mean I had to fucking like the damn flirting.

"Just stop," I told him, gripping the back of my neck.

He lifted his chin, conceding.

I stepped back as Bosco came up.

"We meet again," he said, his southern drawl coming out.

Fuck if I didn't want to punch him, too. I needed to get myself together.

"Hi." Trixie put her hands in the back of her jean pockets, her tits pressing up with the move.

Bosco clicked his tongue. "I can see why, boss." He lifted his chin then strode off.

"Hello, hello, hello," Stiff said from behind us, and we turned. "Look who came back."

"Hey, Stiff." She gave him a soft wave then put her hand back in her pocket.

Stiff appraised her, no doubt liking every inch. "Boss man finally got you here." He shook his head. "He was pissed you didn't show up last night."

At this rate, I was going to have to beat the shit out of every guy here. I wanted to throw her down on the damn grass and fuck her just to show my brothers whom she belonged to. But I wouldn't do it, at least not yet. She needed a little more warming up ... or a lot more.

"Stiff," I warned.

For motherfuckers who had secrets locked deep inside them, this shit—spreading my shit—needed to stop, or I'd beat the hell out of them. Then again, I had never really brought a chick here as mine, so this was an adjustment for all of us.

He held his hands up in surrender. "I speak only the truth." He turned to Trixie. "Keep him happy. He gets cranky." He winked at her then strode off.

"More than he already is?" she grumbled then turned to me. "What now?"

"Let's get some beer in ya. See if you can get that stick outta your ass."

Her hands flew to her hips as her hip jutted out. Fuck, that was sexy. "I do not have a stick up my ass, thank you very much."

I pulled her flush with my body, pressing her into my erection. "That attitude of yours fucking makes my cock hard."

She rolled her eyes.

"You roll your eyes again, and I'm spanking your ass right here in front of everyone."

"You wouldn't." Her hand flew to my chest, pressing against me.

"Fuck yeah, I would."

She flushed red. This time, there was no way I was going soft. The kiss was wet, hard, and brutal. The moment she relaxed into me, I pulled away. Fucking loved her pliant against me, but if I didn't stop, we'd be fucking.

"Let me introduce you to everyone."

She only nodded, her eyes a bit glazed. Fuck me, I was screwed.

"Okay, I've met a Boner, Stiff, Bosco, and Hooch. They call you Spook or Boss man. What's up with all the names?"

I wrapped my arm around her shoulders. Surprisingly, she didn't stop me.

"Road names. We each get one when we become a member."

She bit her bottom lip then let it pop out from her teeth. "So, why do you have two?"

Giving her a soft squeeze, I led her over to the fire pit where several brothers sat, drinking beer. "I only have Spook officially. Boss man is really only for the shop, but it's been catching on more lately. I answer to both."

"So why Spook?"

Stiff walked up, clamping his hand on my shoulder before moving to a nearby chair. "Yeah, Spook, why don't you tell the woman?"

Boner groaned. "Fucking hate this story."

Stiff chuckled. "You would, brother." He turned to me. "Want me to tell it?"

I stared him down, but he kept the smile on his face. "No."

"What? Now I'm even more curious," Trixie said, turning to me fully.

I looked up, catching sight of a couple of stars in the night's sky. "Dipshit over there"—I pointed to Boner—"thought it would be a fantastic idea to get tattoos when we were piss-ass drunk. We were supposed to pick each other's pieces, not telling the other."

"Why in the hell would you do that?" Trixie asked.

I shrugged. "Stupid drunk." I held out my arm, displaying my intricate sleeve. "What do you see here?"

She looked down. "Roses, skulls, and snakes."

"Vipers," I corrected. "What you do not see is the goofy-ass ghost tattoo that Boner thought would be hilarious. It was so damn cartoony the brothers teased me about how spooky it wasn't. Hence, Spook."

"I thought it would be because of some stealth you had on sneaking into places or something," Trixie said.

I chuckled. "I'm not that lucky."

She turned to Boner. "What did you get?"

I burst out laughing. Boner's happened to be really bad.

"Asshole here put an erect cock above my real cock."

Trixie erupted with laughter so strong it caught me off guard. "Let me see."

"Fuck no!" I snapped. No way in hell would I allow that shit.

Her eyes danced. "Oh, come on."

Boner rose.

"You pull your cock out, I'll beat the fuck out you," I warned, dead serious.

Trixie would see no cocks other than mine.

"You have to be special to see it," Boner chided, winked, and then sat back down.

"What? That leaves me out?"

The easy banter between Boner and Trixie should have set me at ease, but it didn't sit right with me. *Fuck.*

EIGHT

TRIX

WELL, THIS WAS HOW CADE LIVED. We sat in lawn chairs that I had to say were very comfortable around a fire pit, the heat taking off the chill of the crisp night air. Cade sat to one side of me while Stiff sat on the other. He hadn't given up his teasing over the last hour, and feeling the waves coming off Cade, Stiff would be lucky to have all of his teeth before the night was over.

It was strange, though. Cade had been acting so damn possessive over me, making my stomach flutter. I, of course, kept zapping those fucking butterflies, because I had no expectations of this lasting more than a couple of days, maybe a week or two.

His brothers were easy to talk to. Finding out the reason for Spook's name was funny, but even more so was Boner's. Glimpsing at his tattoo would be hilarious, but I really had no need to see his dick.

"So, you run Sirens?" Stiff asked.

"Yep. Owned it for five years now. It's my baby." Speaking of which …

I pulled out my phone to find a text from Jett. *Everything is fine.* Not that I thought it wouldn't be, but I had never left the club as much as I'd done since coming in contact with Cade.

I would never tell him this, but I liked taking a break from it. I spent my time always on the go, go, go. Hanging out here, I got to take a nice breather. A bit of calm amongst the storm of my life.

"You gonna hook us up with some new mouses?" Stiff asked.

"Mouses?" What the hell was the deal with these guys and mouses?

"Yeah, girls who like action."

Cade chuckled beside me as the pieces started falling in place.

"I own a strip club, not a brothel." In the TV shows, I had never heard the guys call the hookers, whores, or whoever, mouses. To each their own.

"Here, we have mouses and ol' ladies." I turned to Cade, listening. "Ol' ladies are the brothers' women. Right now, we don't have too many of those since most of the guys are single. There are a few, though."

"Great." I rolled my eyes.

Stiff laughed. "You know we got girls here from Sirens."

I scanned the area, trying to figure out who in the hell was here. I didn't see anyone.

"Don't know their names, but none of them said they're your Nanette. Two of them did say they worked at Sirens, though."

"Who?"

I looked to the far end of the grassy area. From the side view, I could now see Tab on her knees, giving one of the biker dudes a blow job. Nice. What in the fuck was wrong with these women? To each their own.

"Easy, wildcat."

No way would I go over there while she mouth-fucked; however, she could be my key to finding Nanette. Sure, I had lied to Cade about letting it go, but from the look in his eyes, he didn't believe me for a second.

"That one of your girls?" Spook asked, tipping his beer toward Tab.

He'd given me a beer, too, and I'd been holding it by the neck for the past hour. I'd never been big on alcohol, and I definitely wanted to keep my wits about me around people I didn't know.

I nodded. "Tab. I'll talk to her when her mouth isn't full."

Stiff spewed his sip of beer out of his mouth, and I jumped closer to Cade, getting away from the spray.

"What the hell?" I complained.

"That shit's funny, Trixie."

"Trix. I go by Trix," I corrected.

"Nah, you're Trixie," Boner said, and I shook my head. He held his hand up. "It is what it is. Get the fuck over it."

I didn't remember much about Ben, or Boner, during school, only surface stuff. I never liked him the way I had Cade. Still, he seemed rougher now, more take charge. Add that in with his looks, and he was a handsome man. Not as hot as Cade, but still.

Tab rose, kissed the guy on the mouth, and then strutted away.

"I'll be back." Neither Cade nor Stiff stopped me as I made my way through the grass. "Tab," I called out, and she turned quickly, her eyes widening in definite surprise.

"Trix, what are you doing here?" Her words were fast and anxious as she quickly wiped her mouth. I didn't give a shit about her being at Vipers. Whatever she did outside of work was her business.

"Visiting. Is Nanette here?"

It didn't surprise me when she snapped her mouth shut. I had assumed all the girls knew I lent Nanette the money. I waited for the day when one of my girls had enough balls to say something. So far, that hadn't happened.

I stepped closer. "Is she here?"

"I …" She covered her mouth with her hand.

Oh, fuck this shit. I grabbed her tightly around her bicep, giving enough force for her to know I meant business.

"Tell me," I growled. I felt heat at my back, but I didn't turn around because the smell of Cade fell upon me. "Now, Tab. Is she here?"

She shook her head. "She's supposed to be, but she didn't show."

"Where is she?"

"Trix, I don't know. I've seen her here a couple of times, but that's it. We don't talk or anything like that."

That, I could believe.

When tears sprang to her eyes, I let her arm go, stepping back into Cade's heat. I ignored it.

"You call me if you hear from her."

She nodded.

"You working tonight?"

"No."

"Okay, then, have fun."

Tab's eyes grew as she nodded then raced off.

I turned to Cade. "What?"

"Thought you were giving up."

I shrugged. "Might as well ask if I'm here. I need to pee."

He pointed to the clubhouse door. "In, down the hall you were in before, and to the left."

I sidestepped, but he stepped back in front of me. He brought his hand to my chin and lifted it until my eyes met his.

"Wanna fuck you."

I smirked. "Later." I went up on my tiptoes, kissed his lips, and then strode away quickly, no doubt shocking the shit out him.

He didn't chase me, so I figured it was all good. It actually felt a little empowering surprising the big guy. Why? I didn't want to think about that.

The clubhouse climbed with people as the music pumped through the speakers. Laughter spread throughout as some of the guys Spook introduced me to lifted their chins in recognition while several of the women scowled at me. I noticed the difference. The difference between the mouses and the ol' ladies. Where the mouses had barely any clothes on, the ol' ladies did. They were classy yet still very sexy. I could tag each one.

I made my way through the crowd, finally finding the bathroom. I had one just like this at Sirens; except, this one had five stalls with doors and three sinks. Shock hit me at how clean the men kept it.

I went in, going about my business, and was coming out to wash my hands when a buxom blonde strode through the door. By the look of her nonexistent clothes, she had mouse written all over her. Whatever.

I continued washing my hands, looking in the mirror and checking my no longer there lip-gloss. I'd gone light tonight, as I did most nights, but I did pay attention to my eyes. I wanted that pop with liner and lots of mascara.

"You know you'll be gone tomorrow," the voice said as I turned to her.

"Pardon?"

She stepped closer, a mischievous gleam in her eye. "He doesn't want you. He'll fuck you tonight. Then I'll be in his bed tomorrow."

I rested my hip against the sink as I dried my hand with a paper towel. "Is that so?"

She licked her lips. "He always comes back to me."

I could see why. Beauty, she had it. As for the brain department, I couldn't make that call yet.

"Great." I shrugged, but on the inside, my stomach turned. The thought of him with someone else didn't sit right. I shouldn't care, but I didn't like it. Not one little bit. I wouldn't let her know that, though. I wouldn't give her the satisfaction of getting under my skin, because that would be playing directly into her hands. Not happening.

"Great?" She ran her fingers through her hair. "You won't change him."

Okay, whatever. Like I would even put the effort into that.

I tossed the towel into the trash.

"Everyone thinks they're gonna be the one to snag Spook, but no one will." Her eyes gleamed.

"Except you, of course." I crossed my arms over my chest, needing to put them somewhere yet not wanting to let my guard down for a minute, especially with this crazy bitch. Wringing her neck would be too easy.

"I'm the only one who makes him happy."

Yep, crazy.

I shook my head, proceeding toward the door. No way was I playing this game.

A hand came out, grabbing my arm. I turned quickly, dislodging her grasp and pushing her into the door with my hand at her throat, arm extended straight.

Her eyes widened in panic as I gave it a sharp squeeze. I made sure my fingers were on just the right point to inhibit her air. I might not have strong muscle behind me, but I'd been taught how to defend myself.

My arms flexed as I kept my hold tight while she franticly tried to remove my arm to get away.

"You *do not* put your hands on me. You have an issue with Spook, fucking deal with it. It does not involve me. Do you understand?"

I squeezed again when she didn't answer. Instead, she flailed and scratched me with her nails. It hurt, but I pushed it back, not letting that show a bit, another thing my father taught me well.

I released only enough to lift her head before slamming it into the door. This bitch was seriously stupid. Hopefully, that would knock some sense into her.

"Do." Slam. "You." Slam. "Understand?"

"I got it," she mumbled, not sure how to take me.

I wanted to laugh, but I didn't. I smiled, though.

"Good. I don't give a flying fuck what you do, but you leave me the hell out of it." I meant every word. I needed to bring my gun next time.

Listen to me. *Next time?* I needed to get the hell out of here.

With one more squeeze, I released her.

She gasped for breath, scrambling away from me and tripping over her heels, just to fall back to the floor.

"You're fucking crazy," she choked out.

I smiled, opening the door. "No, bitch, you are."

As the door clattered behind me, I looked at my arms. The fucking bitch drew blood, but I didn't want to go back in the bathroom to deal with Spook's tail.

As I wiped the red iron, it just smeared. The cuts weren't bad, but I needed to get them cleaned up. Bitch must have had points on her damn nails.

I headed to the bar, moving through the throng of people. Surely, they could give me some paper towels or something.

The kid who had followed me to the clubhouse stood behind the bar, handing out beers. His eyes hit me then my arms. "What happened?"

"Little misunderstanding. Can I get a towel and some water?"

He nodded as he pulled out his phone, punching in something.

"Girlfriend?" I asked as I watched him.

"Spook."

"Why the hell did you text him?"

He shrugged. "You're his girl. You're hurt." He pulled the paper towels from the bottom of the bar then handed me a bottle of water. "He'd be pissed if I didn't."

I gripped the bottle, opening it then pouring some on a towel. "I'm not *his* girl."

"Whatever." The guy left as I cleaned myself quickly.

The door to the clubhouse burst open with a heavy crash, and my eyes flew to it.

Cade.

His eyes were glittering with anger as he found me at the bar, predatorily stalking my way. People moved, no one daring to block him. Part of me wanted to cower, but no way would I let that happen. Instead, I straightened my shoulders and lifted my chin.

He grabbed my arms, though not hard, and then turned them, inspecting me.

"What the fuck happened?"

It was over. No need to deal with the bullshit.

"Misunderstanding. It's all taken care of."

His eyes turned intense, demanding. Fuck, it sent my body aflame.

"What. The. Fuck. Happened?" Each word was clipped.

I met his stare, not saying anything. I would not let him intimidate me.

"Tell me." Unfortunately, he didn't feel the urge to step back.

I could feel eyes on me from all around the room. Everything stopped around us: the music, people dancing, talking. I really didn't like that shit. I breathed out, wanting the focus off me.

"Some bitch in the bathroom had a problem with me, said you'd be done with me tomorrow and go back to her. I ignored her until she put her hands on me. Once that happened, I had to let her know that no one touches me like that. It's done with. I'm fine. Ease the testosterone." And he did ooze that shit. I could smell it. Damn, it turned me on.

"Who?"

"She didn't tell me her name."

He released my arm, his focus on searching the room. "Show me who she is."

As his body vibrated, I felt the need to calm him, so I stepped up close, putting my hand on his arm. His eyes came to my hands.

"It's okay, Cade. I handled it."

He covered my hand with his hot one, sending sparks up my arm. "Anyone touches you, Trixie—I mean, fucking anyone—they deal with me."

A thrill coursed through my veins. I liked it. Did that make me a freak? I didn't care.

"I get that, but I handled it."

"No, Trixie. This is my club, and you're my girl. No one touches what's mine."

I full-out shivered, even if I disagreed with the *my* girl thing.

I looked out into the crowd, pretending to look for the woman. I really didn't know what Cade would do to her, but it wasn't worth it. My eyes hit hers. She gasped, widening her eyes. Damn, she gave herself away.

"Stacy," Cade growled before leaving my side.

I should have run after him, should have stopped him, but I did neither. I stayed still. He was right. This was his club, and he did things his own way. If he tried to tell me how to run my business, I'd be pissed as shit.

Cade grabbed the woman by the arm, saying a few things to her. Her skin paled as he led her through the crowd, escorting her out the main door.

I turned back to the bar to find the kid who followed me here staring.

"What?"

"Told you that you were his girl."

I rolled my eyes.

NINE

TRIX

"**F**OLD." I THREW MY CARDS INTO THE middle of the table while the guys around me smiled. Seven of them: Stiff, Bosco, Boner, Dawg, Hooch, who Cade introduced me to earlier, then the new guys; Worm and Skid. Each of them had their own sex appeal, but their names … Worm? Seriously? And Skid? The first thing I thought of were skid marks on underwear and hoped that wasn't how he had gotten his name. I hadn't asked. After learning about Spook's name, I realized anything went.

While sitting at the bar, Stiff came in declaring a round of poker. Some guys cheered, others hadn't given a shit.

I hadn't seen Spook for about ten minutes since taking the woman away. I had no clue where to. I stayed at the bar, taking in the surroundings. When Stiff called me over to join, I didn't want to go. I had actually thought of taking off, but when he told me not to be a *schmuck*, I said fuck it, let's play. I'd show him schmuck, alright.

We each put twenty bucks in and got a stack of chips. I now sat at the table, all eyes on me, everyone thinking they had just taken my twenty bucks. They were in for a rude awakening.

"Folding already." Stiff chuckled, his pinky finger tapping on the table absently.

I'd been watching for five rounds, getting a feel for my opponents. The finger tap meant Stiff had a good hand. When it was bad, he pulled in his bottom lip, sucking it into his mouth. Those were the only two tells I could pick up, yet it had only been a short time.

"Yep." I leaned back and sipped my Diet Coke.

"Never gonna win if you keep foldin'," Bosco's deep voice rang out as he smirked.

His tells were a bit harder. His eyes were his cue for a good hand. On a good hand, his eyes would slip from the pot to his cards. He did it so nonchalantly most people would miss it. I wasn't most people. For a bad hand, the focus went to his mouth. With the slightest tick on the left side of his lip—again, so fast if you weren't paying attention—you would have no hope. He had obviously been playing for a long time and knew his shit. I liked him already.

I shrugged. "Didn't say I was in to win. I'm just killing time." In actuality, I was having a fucking blast. It had been a long time since I played, but when I did, I always enjoyed the game. The thrill, learning the opponents' tells, what they meant—all of it got me high. It was the challenge, the high I'd forgotten I loved.

"Spook'll be back soon," Boner cut in, stomping out his cigarette and blowing a puff of smoke into the air.

"Whatever." I really didn't care in that moment if he came in at all. The joy of the game sent me soaring.

I looked over at Dawg. His right brow lifted as he tossed in a chip. He had a good hand. With a bad one, he stayed blank.

"Yeah, whatever." Bosco chuckled, tossing in a chip. "I call."

Bosco, Boner, and Dawg were the only ones in this hand. They laid their cards down. Boner only had a pair of tens, while Dawg had two pair—threes and fives. When Bosco laid down his flush of hearts, the guys groaned as Bosco chuckled, pulling all the chips from the center into his pile.

"Way to go," I encouraged, tossing my cards to Boner who started shuffling and dealing.

"That's how ya play the game." He smiled, the beard and mustache almost hiding it. "Taking lessons?" he pushed.

"Oh, yeah." I gave a soft wink.

He sat up a little straighter. Guys were so gullible sometimes.

The next round, I had shit cards—a pair of fours. I knew I wouldn't win the pot, but I played it out, keeping focused on Hooch, Worm, and Skid. Hooch didn't hide his cards from his face; anyone could read him like a book. He was a horrible bluffer. Worm and Skid had some eye contact thing going on with each other that I was trying to work out when Boner called.

I laid out my hand.

"Oh!" Bosco chided. "Baby, you've gotta have more than a pair to win poker." His words had a knowing tone to them.

I turned, raising my brow at him. He shook his head and tossed his cards to the center of the table.

The time had come. I was ready.

I still couldn't figure out Worm and Skid, but it was time to get this show on the road. The thrill fed my adrenaline. Keeping it in check proved to be difficult, but I did.

Once the cards landed in front of me, I lifted the corners slightly, seeing an ace of diamonds and of spades, two of hearts, five of clubs, and jack of hearts. Okay, a pair. I kept the jack and tossed in the five and the two. My new cards came. A jack of spades and a three of clubs. Nice. Two pair. Not the best hand, but not the worst.

I checked the guys. Stiff bit his lip. Bosco's eyes moved from the center pot to his cards. Dawg's brow tipped up. Hooch's eyes squinted in disgust. Skid tapped a chip on the table as Worm sat perfectly still.

I shrugged, tossing in two chips. "I'm in."

"Oh, she plays!" Bosco teased to my smile. Yep, *she* was playing now. Really playing.

Boner tossed in chips into the center, grabbing another chip and twirling it. His tell was so obvious I tried not to laugh. Clockwise, he had a good hand; counter-clockwise, he had a shitty one. Currently, he turned it counter-clockwise. Why he bet, I had no idea. He probably didn't want me to show him up or something stupidly macho.

Bosco tossed in like I knew he would, as did Dawg. Skid looked at Worm then tossed in, but Hooch and Worm folded with Hooch leaning back in his seat.

I needed to bluff. I had great cards, but I needed them to think I had better. I held my fingers straight. I scratched the table with my middle finger absently when I had a shitty hand or was nervous. I'd been called out on it many times. I did my best to keep mindful of it. Everything happened subconsciously, though. If I didn't really think about it, I would show it without realizing it.

I raised two, keeping my eyes on the guys still in. Boner stayed, chucking in his chip. I didn't know why when his hand was shit. Stiff, on the other hand, kept that pinky tapping. I kept my breathing even.

He smirked, tossing in his chips. "Call."

Skid bailed, tossing his cards to the center.

Fuck. Here goes nothing.

I laid my two pair with the lonely three down.

Stiff's eyes narrowed. He flipped his cards down, throwing them to the table, only showing one pair of sevens. "Motherfucker," he growled.

I smiled.

"Did you cheat?" he accused.

"How in the hell could I have cheated?" I reached into the middle of the pot and began stacking up my chips.

I caught Bosco looking at my cleavage, a smirk playing on his lips. Boobs, gotta love them.

"I don't know. You just folded five games in a row then bam!" Stiff protested. The man did not like to lose.

"Beginners luck." I continued stacking until Boner chuckled. "What?"

"Nothing, nothing at all." His smile told me differently. He remembered. I knew he did, but he didn't say anything.

When I turned to Bosco, his tipped lip, along with the shaking of the head, told me he knew, too. They knew exactly who my father was, but neither of them were saying anything. I had to wonder why not.

"Fuck, that made me hard," Skid said, his hand going under the table to adjust his pants, I guessed.

I tipped my brow. "Me winning made you hard?"

"Fuck, yeah. You do that again, and I'll show ya." His deep chocolate brown eyes matched his hair. His chiseled cheekbones made his face look stern, but the scar over his right eye caught me. It was long and angry, marring up his face, yet it gave him that dangerous look. The untouchable, sexy one.

"What was that, Skid?" Cade's stern voice came from behind me.

I jumped. I didn't smell him or hear him, nothing. I looked up from my seat to see his eyes directed at Skid.

"Oh, your boy here was just telling ol' Trixie how hard she made him," Boner said as he and Bosco laughed.

Cade did not. No, his eyes narrowed as his fists clenched. As sexy as it was to have a guy want to beat up every man who looked my way, it also wasn't going to happen.

"Down, boy." My words only made Boner, Bosco, and now Stiff laugh deepen.

"Yeah, *boy*," Bosco chided.

I noticed Worm just sat there, taking everything in, not reacting. Strange.

Cade cut the group with a menacing look, and I sighed. If I wanted to keep playing poker, I couldn't have Cade going all ape-shit over nothing. I needed to calm him. Lord, what was wrong with me?

I reached up, touching Cade's arm, and his muscle tensed. "Come have a seat. Remember? *Just live in the fucking moment*," I mimicked his deep voice with the words he told me earlier.

His eyes flashed with lust. My core clenched.

He lifted my chin as he bent down. I then lost all sense of reality when his lips attacked mine. I had to do something with my hands, so I gripped his shirt, his smooth leather brushing my thumbs. Damn, this man could kiss.

When he pulled away, I registered all the whoops and hollers going on around me. I blinked back the fog that was Cade.

"We fucking get it." Boner snickered, lighting up. "She's fucking yours."

I moved away from Cade's hand, turning to Boner. "Afraid to tell ya, I'm nobody's but my own."

That apparently was the wrong thing to say, because Cade lifted me into the air by my armpits, slamming me hard against his rock hard body. I grabbed his shoulders, trying to get my feet to balance from the impact, having trouble doing so.

"What the …?"

Lips, tongue, pulsing between my thighs—I couldn't register anything else. My head clouded, my breathing forgotten, as I tried to keep up with Cade's lips, but his were too powerful, too knowing, too determined. He controlled everything. Nothing existed for that moment except him and me.

He ripped his lips away, and I inhaled deep, attempting to get air into my lungs. My chest seized at the intense look in his eyes.

"Trixie, not fucking with you. Say that shit again, and the entire room gets a shot at your ass."

Oh, hell no. There was no way in hell I would allow his brothers to spank my ass. Not. Going. To. Happen.

"Fuck you," I grumbled, trying to push him away. "What took you so long with Stacy?" I asked, feeling the rage burn through me. I mean, he took forever out there with her. Who knew if she had given him head or touched him in any way. And shit, I had just let him kiss me.

"That what this is about?" he asked, tightening his grip. I wiggled.

"Fuck off," I retorted.

He leaned into my ear. "Gave her to a brother to get her off Vipers' property. She was a pain in the ass, and it took a little longer than I anticipated. Didn't fucking touch her."

"Yeah, right," I replied.

"Yeah, exactly right."

I gave him a shove, but he didn't budge.

"You keep pushing away"—his hand came between my legs, and I groaned— "but your body says a totally different thing. You're fucking mine, Trixie. Always have been."

I instantly snapped my legs shut, trapping his hand inside. If he thought I would sit back and allow this shit, he was as crazy as that bitch Stacy. I opened my mouth, but he spoke first.

"Stop," he ordered. Anger pulsed through my veins like hot lava. "I'll give you a way to work out that anger later … unless you want me to fuck you in front of everyone," he said, leaning into my ear. "I'm totally fine with that."

My damn heart picked up speed. I didn't want him to know it, but Cade being Cade, he did.

He smirked. "I'm gonna let you go. Play your game."

I went to war inside my head. While I did enjoy the game and the challenge, I wasn't going to put up with his shit.

"I'm leaving."

His grip tightened as I struggled.

"Let me go."

He sighed, turned me around, sat down, and then placed me on his lap, his arm around me like a steel band.

"You fucking little shit, Cade, let me up."

His dick got harder with each move I made. My body wanted him, the traitorous bitch.

I moved to elbow him, but his other arm came up, pinning my arms behind my back. I had no clue how in the hell he moved so fast without using his other arm, but he did. He growled, "I'm pulling off your fucking jeans, spreading you out on the table, and giving each guy three swats for interrupting their game."

I stilled. His tone left no room for argument. It wasn't a threat. No, it was a promise that sent chills up my spine.

"Exactly. One fucking more, Trixie, and it's happening. I'm done."

I'd pushed him all the way to his limit. I knew I needed to back down. I didn't want to, but I knew, if I didn't, he would follow through.

"Fine," I clipped out harshly. I may have been giving in, but I would let him know I didn't like it.

I relaxed my body, and he let go of me. Then I wiggled my ass on his lap. His hands bit into my hip, and I ignored him, turning back to the table.

"Sorry about that. Let's play."

Play I did, with purpose and determination. Having Cade under me, I ignored my throbbing need for him, keeping my eye on the game.

Hooch went out first—no surprise there—followed by Worm, Dawg, Skid, and then Boner. Stiff, Bosco, and myself were the only ones left. I itched to take them down.

When I pulled a full house with three jacks and two queens, I bet high, knowing I had a winning hand. Bosco bowed out, but Stiff couldn't. He met my bet, tossing in all of his chips, still tapping that pinky.

Not one to back down, I saw his bet, flipping my cards to show him.

"Fucking hell!" Stiff roared, tossing out his four kings. He had a damn good hand, but not good enough. Hell yes! "You've got to be shitting me."

The guys roared with laughter. I even found myself doing it, too. Cade's body shook with his amusement. Stiff yelled across the bar for a beer, which caused Lee to come rushing over quickly with a fresh one. He downed most of it in seconds.

Bosco gathered the cards, lit a cigarette, and then dealt them out. "Last round. All in," he announced, catching everyone's attention.

I had a fifty-fifty shot. There were no tells to notice. It was a flat out, no holds barred, deal of the deck. Adrenaline pumped through my veins, lighting me on fire.

"Hell, yeah." There was no way I could give up this challenge. None.

A little voice inside my head whispered, *fucking idiot*, but I pushed it aside.

Bosco lifted his chin in what felt like approval, and my heart filled with pride.

Cade began stroking my leg, sending tingles with each movement. The anger from before brushed away as I let the energy of the moment fill me. Damn, I missed this shit.

Bosco dealt. I lifted the corners, finding hearts—three of them: an ace, king, and a jack. The other two were shit cards. I tossed in the two shits, hoping luck was on my side.

Two cards fell on top, but I didn't look at them. They didn't matter, because it was what it was. Instead of looking, I stared at Bosco. He looked at his cards, but this time, he kept his face impassive.

When he looked up, he asked, "Did you look?"

I shook my head.

The tension sparked like a live wire. I felt jazzed as hell. The high captivated me like a drug better than I ever had. The money didn't matter; I couldn't give a shit about that. The rush of the game became so much more important to me. Such a big part of my childhood involved cards. To have that back—the happy parts—was fucking awesome.

"Turn," he called.

I turned my cards, not looking down, my heart thumping out of my chest. I looked at his turned over cards, and my heart stopped. A straight flush, ten through six of diamonds. How in the hell had he pulled that out of his ass?

Shock hit me like a mallet. My eyes went to my cards, and all the air left my lungs as a smile crept to my lips.

"A fucking royal flush, baby!" I yelled, pounding my hands hard on the table, the joy hitting me like the weight of an elephant. It felt so damn good.

I ended up with an ace through ten of hearts, a royal damn flush!

Bosco sat back in his seat, looking shocked as hell. I was, too. I had the fucking luck.

Stiff sat dumbstruck while Boner heaved out a laugh.

Skid started pushing all the chips my way when something hit my gut hard, fading my laughter. I didn't want their money. For some reason, I felt bad. I'd never felt bad after winning, but part of me felt deceptive in a way.

Fuck it. I pushed the chips back into the middle. "I'm not taking your money."

Bosco's brow lifted.

"Look, my father taught me to play poker." I sucked in a deep breath, not knowing which way this shit would go. "You may know him. He goes by the Colonel. He's the best damn card player and taught me everything I know."

Bosco's eyes changed into what I thought might be approval.

Cade banded his arm around my waist, his chin resting on my shoulder. It felt right. His cheeks were tugged up in a grin.

The guys began talking, but for some reason, I kept my eyes on Bosco. When his face broke out in a wide smile, hidden by his beard and mustache, I began to breathe.

"You've got my vote," he said as Cade squeezed me harder.

The relief instantly died. *His vote? This was a test?* A test to find out if I'd tell them about my father. Fucking shit.

"You've got to be shitting me!" I yelled, standing so fast I broke Cade's grip.

"And that's our cue to get the fuck out of here." Cade bent down, pressed his shoulder to my stomach, and lifted me up. The air in my body came out in a whoosh.

TEN

SPOOK

"**P**UT ME DOWN!" SHE SCREAMED, smacking my ass from her upside down position. I had to admit, I liked having her ass right in my face.

When she started kicking ferociously, I hit her plump ass hard, followed by two more in quick succession. Enough of that shit.

"You spanked me! You've got to be kidding me."

My keys scraped my hand as I pulled them out of my pocket. I unlocked the door then stepped through with a still not happy Trixie. I plopped her down on her feet, and she stormed toward the door as I slammed and locked it.

"Calm down, wildcat."

She slammed into me, no fear, just rage burrowing through her. "I can't believe your fucking guys were testing me! Who the fuck does that? Why the fuck did they do that?"

I was a little surprised by her anger. Sure, the guys were challenging her, wanting her to come clean on her own. I knew what they were doing, and I didn't see a problem with it.

In our world, the president having a woman, a real woman who lay beside him every night, was important to get right. If Trixie was a conniving piece of shit like her father, the guys wouldn't trust her and would have shit to talk about her sharing my bed. And while I wouldn't accept any of that bullshit, I also understood it.

My brothers didn't need someone whispering stupid shit in my ear that could get us killed or locked up. While I cleaned up the mess all those years ago, it didn't mean we were as clean as bleach. No, we had our ties. We had our markers. The guys needed to trust that the woman lying next to me, whispering in my ear, was smart with grit.

My brothers knew I was serious as shit about keeping Trixie this time, so I couldn't blame them one bit. However, I knew Trixie wouldn't disappoint me.

Her excitement during the game sucked me in like a drug. I could feel it coming off her while she sat on my lap with her hot heat. While she didn't show much, her heat told me how hot as hell she was.

"Wildcat," I tried, but she kept going.

"I mean, it's not like I'm staying with you. I'm not gonna be part of *your world* as you call it. There's no need for it." She started gasping in breath like she couldn't get it into her lungs.

I wrapped my arms around her, pulling her securely to me. More was going on here than just a simple little test. Something big, it felt like.

"Calm down."

She balled her hands into fists and started hitting me. Her eyes were pissed, yet something deeper resided inside them.

"I will not calm down. It's always a test. Always. My whole fucking life has been one big test." She screamed so loudly I had no doubt my brothers heard over the music.

Wrapping her wrists with one hand and clutching her body to mine with the other, she twisted as the anger poured off her.

"Tell me what the fuck is going on!" I yelled back.

"What's going on?" She shook her head, her body starting to tremble, but this time, her words were choked when they came out. "My father always tested me … every single moment he could. I couldn't ever be good enough for him. Then tonight, I'm having fun, really having fun, Cade. For the first time in a really long time, I let the rush of the game carry me away, and it was just a test. Something for your guys to determine, what? If I'm good enough for a man who doesn't even really want me?" She shook her head hard, pushing against my chest as anger bubbled. "I'm leaving. I'm getting the fuck out of here, going back to Sirens, and forgetting all this shit."

I didn't let her go. No way in hell.

"Trixie, you're not going anywhere. Take some fucking breaths so we can talk this shit out."

She shook her head, looking down. "I …" It sounded as if she were fucking crying. Surely, that couldn't happen.

"Trixie," I called, and slowly, she raised her head to me. Sure as shit, tears filled her eyes.

"I can't do this, Cade." She shook her head. "I can't."

"What exactly can't you do?"

"This thing between us … I can't. I need to go." This time, she pleaded, but there was no way in hell she'd step out of my sight.

"No."

She breathed out a resigned, deep sigh. "Fine, then just fuck me so I can leave." She sounded so damn wiped out, like all the strength had left her. Where had the fight gone?

I didn't understand it at all. Not from the fireball that came into my office, demanding to find a woman who stole from her. She was lost, unable to put it back together. Regardless, we would get past this. My little Trixie had some deep-rooted feelings. I hated that for her. I had no doubt her father was an ass to her. She had more than likely given up trying to be the woman who could make him proud.

"Babe," I whispered in a tone she hadn't yet heard from me, one I didn't know I had possessed until that moment. It caught her attention as she stilled in my arms, looking up at me. "You talk to your father much?"

Her breath hitched. "Not if I can help it." That was good. I didn't want to do this shit here, but it needed to get out and be done.

I pulled her over to the bed, in between my legs. Her back rested to my front as I held on to her tight.

108 | RYAN MICHELE

"I did something a long time ago that caused this test." Fuck, I didn't want to tell her this shit. Never wanted to tell her. She deserved so much better than me, but I didn't fucking care. She was the same old Trixie as back then, only with a few scars from over the years. *Mine.*

"I'm telling you this because you aren't some fuck to me. This isn't some game of playing you for a fool. This isn't me trying to get you in my good graces, just to break your heart all over again."

She dropped her head down to her chest. I knew I hit a mark. Tonight wasn't supposed to be this deep, but fuck it. I might as well get this shit out in the open.

I shifted, resting my back against the headboard. I needed to hold her while I delivered this blow.

"Leaving you was the hardest thing I ever did. And, Trixie, I've done some hard things in my life, but giving you up tore me apart."

She harrumphed. "Yeah, right. You were fucking girls left and right after me."

True, but she had gotten one thing wrong.

"Only because I couldn't have you. I know it's shitty, but it's the truth."

"Whatever." She didn't believe me, but maybe after the next part, she would.

"When I was a kid, I knew my place would be in this club. Someday, I'd be the president and follow in my father's footsteps. Unfortunately, my father's steps were caked in so much shit no one in this club was safe. The Vipers were drowning because he started a side business. Some members of the club knew about it, while others were kept in the dark." This would hit her; I just knew it. "My father got in the business of kidnapping and selling women to overseas men who paid a shit load for them."

She snapped her head around just as I thought she would. Trixie's mouth hung open, but no words came out.

"I knew all about it. I saw shit you don't need to hear about." The memories of it flooded my head. I pushed them as far out as I could. That dirt never came off, no matter how much you cleaned it. It still followed you until the day you died.

"At eighteen, I made a plan. I didn't want to be associated with a club that dealt in women, but I had a problem because my father refused to let me out. So I had to get the club out and into clean businesses. Also, I needed to get rid of my father because I knew he wouldn't ever back down.

"I needed to find someone to take over the girls. With what my father had going, he had to supply, which meant if he didn't, they would come after the club. I was young, but I paid attention to the world around me with a keen eye. Only one man around here I could see helping me. He had the power to do what needed to be done."

Even though I told Boner I was telling her this shit, I didn't want to, but she needed to know. Know who she was letting into her bed. Despite that, I wouldn't let go of her.

"The Colonel took over the business."

She stilled then fully turned in my arms, the color completely leaving, her face now a pasty white. "No way."

"Yeah."

Her eyes were wide in shock. It felt good to know she didn't have a fucking clue about it.

"I gave him the business in exchange for two things: one, protection for my club and, two, that you would never be sold and always protected, which we all still have to this day."

She started to bolt from the bed, but I pulled her to me so that she straddled my legs. Her arms were behind her back.

"Let me the fuck go!" she screamed, her eyes smoldering.

"Trixie, you gotta listen."

"I think I've listened enough. He was going to fucking sell me?" Her words were disbelieving as anger pulled from her depths.

"Trixie, I didn't know for sure what the fuck he was capable of. He intended to take over a business that kidnapped women then sold them as sex slaves. I knew he was your father, and it fucking scared the shit out of me that he'd do it. I had to take out my old man to make the plan all work. I couldn't keep my eyes on you and deal with all my club shit."

"So, you mean to tell me that you gave my father a sex slave business in exchange for him not selling me off?"

"And protection for my club and you. Trixie, I didn't want the business, but it brings in millions of dollars. The whole thing made me sick as fuck. I couldn't deal with it."

"So why didn't you just shut it down? Why give it away so other women would continue to be hurt?" Her voice turned stern yet broken.

"Told you. The assholes my father got in line with weren't gonna release my club unless they had somewhere else to get the girls. I needed it released, babe. Needed it off radar. The Colonel did that for me. He took it over, providing the girls. We were actually lucky it was that fucking easy, and we all didn't end up dead, which at the time, was a strong possibility. Those fuckers are ruthless. Being an eighteen-year-old kid to them, I had to do what I had to do to gain their trust." That was something I wouldn't discuss with her.

"Then why my father? He's a card shark, for God's sake. He doesn't deal in women." It felt like she was trying to convince herself that all of this was a line of shit, and saying it out loud would accomplish that. She was very much mistaken.

"He had hookers, so moving to that stage didn't come as a hardship for him. He had plenty of women at his disposal at any given time. Being who he is, the women flocked to him because he provided protection to them for a cut of their money."

Trixie pulled away from me. "Just give me a second, Cade." Confusion swarmed in her eyes, her voice soft.

The way she said my name hit me hard, so I reluctantly released her.

She paced the room. Her thumb went to her mouth as she chewed on her nail. She said nothing, just paced. I gave her that time. I laid a lot on her all at once. Taking that in would be tough.

Time stretched out as she continued to do her thing, her mind no doubt a buzz of questions.

When she lifted her face, her eyes met mine.

Trixie came to the bed. "I need to sleep. I can't think about this anymore." She took off her jeans then climbed in. She covered herself up, putting her rigid back to me.

I pressed my chest to her back and wrapped my arms around her. She didn't flinch or move a muscle. She shut down on me. I could feel it.

"Trixie?" I whispered.

"No, Cade. Not right now. I need to sleep," she pleaded.

I kissed the top of her head. "Sleep," I told her.

Several hours later, I felt her body relax into sleep.

ELEVEN

TRIX

*H*IS LIGHT SNORES TOLD ME HE HAD fallen asleep. The arm around my waist relaxed, releasing its tight grip. I waited for what seemed like an eternity before sliding out of bed as quietly as possible.

Being with him came so easily it scared me. Therefore, I picked my offense to play tired. The goal being to get him to sleep then get the fuck out of here. It had better work.

I knew he wouldn't have let me leave earlier. I also knew he told me never to leave the bed, but fuck him. Fighting with him wouldn't have been an option, because I would have lost. He would have done something to make me fall into his world and stay. However, I didn't know who in the hell this man was. He most definitely was not the guy I had lost my virginity to. The worst part was I thought he still had some of that in him.

I hated being wrong.

Quickly and quietly, I put on my jeans before moving toward the door, still keeping an eye on Cade. He remained lying there, naked from the chest up, a sheet covering his lower half. His tattoos that I inspected before were an intricate design that flexed with each breath he took. He looked so damn peaceful, happy even.

I was a fool telling myself my heart couldn't get involved, but it didn't have choice with Cade. From the first moment I'd laid eyes on him, he became my infatuation. Even after he had let me go and through all the pain, I still cared for him. Shit, I even loved him.

Those six months we spent together were the best of my life. My father was there, but not really, always busy doing something.

I had no mother. I'd asked my father about her, but he shot me down every time until I gave up. I had to raise myself. Sure, I had nannies who stayed with me at times, but they never treated me any differently than my father—a burden. Always a burden. Once Cade entered my life, it made the world a little more bearable. Then my world crashed.

The man lying in that bed had lost his mind. *Sex slaves?* I wasn't naive. I knew shit happened in the world, but come on. My father a part of it? It was too much.

His eyes though, spoke of honesty, giving me the same look when we had been kids. Deep in my gut, I believed him, but it was too overwhelming. I needed to get out. I needed space to think, and doing it lying next to Cade proved impossible.

I spotted a side door that had a big illuminated exit sign above it. I opened it. My lucky day. It led right into the parking lot.

I darted to my car, fumbling with my keys to get them out of my pocket. Laughter could be heard through the dark night in the distance as I entered the car. I sat there, my hands shaking, everything weighing on me like an elephant on my shoulders.

I looked in the rearview mirror. My eyes were a bit void. That was scary. I closed them, taking some deep breaths. *I got this.*

I started the engine, pulled out, and had to stop at the big gate. The same man with the goatee came to the window. Needing to play this cool so he would let me out of here, I rolled down the window.

He smiled appraisingly. "Hey, how you doin'?"

"I need out, please," I told him, ignoring his lust-filled eyes.

"You seem a little tense. Not get what you needed from the boss?"

Suck it up, Trix.

I plastered on a sultry smile, biting my bottom lip as suggestively as I could. "Oh, yeah. I'm letting him sleep it off."

"He know you're leavin'?"

I rolled my eyes in exasperation then lied through my goddamned teeth. "Of course. You think he'd let me leave if he didn't want me to?"

He nodded. "Nope, but hard for me to believe he wants you out of his bed."

I leaned forward, no doubt giving him a great view of my tits. "Believe it. Can you open the gate please?" I gave him my best eye flutter bullshit. I'd seen my girls use it to work over a client for bigger tips.

He licked his lips. "Fuck." He raised his hand to the guy above in the tower, stepping back from the car.

The damn gate seemed to take an eternity to open, but as soon as it did, I floored it, getting the fuck away from that nut house.

TOSSING CLOTHES INTO MY BAG, I ran into the bathroom, gathering all my toiletries. I needed to go somewhere Cade couldn't find me, because I had no doubt he would. At the moment, the only person I could trust in my life was myself, because I'd never let myself down. I had Jett, but I could never tell her any of this. My gut told me that I needed to hole up in a hotel for a few days to clear my head.

I grabbed my gun, putting it in my purse, and went to my closet, picking up my small safe. After entering the combination, the metal popped open, displaying another gun along with cash. I stored about three thousand in there. The money would be enough to get a semi-nice place without using a credit card.

Cade was smart. My credit card would be the third thing he checked after checking here and Sirens.

I put everything in the bag making it to the hotel in record time. I checked in under the name Annabelle Jacks then bolted every single lock on the door.

The mid-range hotel sat on the side of town. The walls were painted a universal beige with the carpet a darker tan. A small kitchenette with a fridge and microwave sat on one wall with a large-screened television. The bed looked seriously comfortable, covered in white linens. This place would do fine.

Even lying in bed, I couldn't relax. Everything rattled around in my head. There was too much to think about.

Part of me wanted to go straight to my father and flat-out ask him, but I wasn't stupid. My father had always been a dick. That was his nature. He had zero patience, especially when I got something wrong. Despite that, he had never hit me or hurt me physically in any way.

Believing he had taken over a sex slave operation and was still running it to this day didn't compute. Not to mention, the thought of him selling me as Cade said. Why would he do that? He might not have liked the fact that I wasn't born a boy, but to sell me to some asshole who would do God knows what to me? What father would do that to his child?

Sure, my father had a mysterious aura always surrounding him. He had men he called friends, but with one look at their bulkiness, I knew they were guards. I'd asked once about them, and he told me it was none of my business, so I never asked again. I thought he was a card player; I mean, how else would he have taught me?

When he was teaching me self-defense and giving me a business sense, I had never thought about why he needed the guards. It was just how my life was. Cade said the Colonel had hookers. I didn't know about that.

Then there was the fact that Cade had to even get involved in this in the first place. Did he hurt the girls his father had? Did he treat them like the mouses in his clubhouse? Did he actually help his father sell kidnapped girls? At that thought, the tears fell from my eyes. Everything I thought I knew about Cade was a lie.

I tossed and turned all night and into the morning. I rose from the bed with a heavy head, like I'd been on an all-night bender or something.

I grabbed my phone, seeing thirteen missed calls from Cade, one from Jett, and a whole slew of text messages. The ones from Cade, I ignored, only reading the ones from Jett. Nothing big, just telling me everything went well last night.

I ordered room service and watched movies until the sun set. I turned my phone off completely after the vibrations from Cade calling wouldn't stop.

My damn heart would flutter every time he called, but I wouldn't pick it up. I couldn't trust him. I couldn't trust anyone except Jett to run Sirens.

I texted her, telling her I wouldn't be in tonight, then fell asleep with the gun under my pillow.

I AWOKE TO A BANGING ON the door that jolted me upright and caused my heart to pound.

"Trixie, open the fucking door, or I swear I'll fucking bust it down," Cade's voice rang through the other side.

How in the fuck did he find me? I covered my location and done everything possible to stay hidden. I'd made sure of it.

No light came through the windows, so it had to be night still.

My bare feet hit the plush carpet as I made my way to the door, looking out the peephole. I saw Cade's vein pulse in his neck, anger radiating off him. Not only that, but Boner and Stiff were with him. *Fuck.*

"I know you're fucking in there, Trixie. Open the goddamned door now."

I didn't want to.

I heaved out a big sigh. "Cade, go away. I'm tired. Please leave," I said so softly I didn't know if he heard me.

I pressed my palms to the door to hold me up as a wave of despair hit me. It felt like fifteen years ago when he ignored me. Except, this time, it was worse. I knew what he really felt like now, what he tasted like. Regardless, I couldn't trust him. He'd broken that a long time ago, and now with new information sprung on me I was so damn confused.

"No, open the door."

My heart hurt as it squeezed, and a tear slid down my cheek.

"Cade, go away."

"Trixie, let me in *now.*"

I hit the door hard with my palm, screeching, "I'm done! Whatever sick game you have going on here, I don't want any part of it, Cade Baker. I'm out. Leave now!"

The last part had a crack in my voice that pissed me off.

"Trixie." His voice calming. "This isn't a game, and I'd rather not discuss this through a fucking door where everyone in the damn hallway can hear."

"Just please go."

"Trix," Boner said softly in a voice that was so damn compassionate I almost forgot why I didn't want them inside the room. "Open the door and let us talk to you."

I shook my head, tears falling from my face. I knew they couldn't see, which was a good thing since I didn't cry in front of anyone if I could help it.

"Babe, just open up so we can talk to you," Stiff said, his voice also calm.

"I can't," I told them.

"Why not?" Cade clipped.

"Because I can't trust you, Cade. I can't trust any of you." I couldn't trust anyone in my life. While my gut told me he was being honest with me, that didn't mean I could actually trust him.

"Trixie, you can trust me. Always," Cade said as I rested my forehead on the door.

I wanted that. I wanted to have someone I could count on in my life, but I didn't. All I had was myself, and that sucked.

"No, I can't. I don't know who you are anymore, Cade. I don't know what you're into or what you've done. This story is so farfetched I can't wrap my head around it. Then, with the Colonel involved … I just can't." All of it was too much. I was a damn strong woman, but fuck, talk about bringing a woman down to her knees.

"How can you not trust me? I told you the truth, something I don't tell anyone. Please open the door so we can come in. I can't have everyone hearing me."

"You're not gonna go away, are you?" I relented.

"No, babe. Open up."

I lifted my head from the door and pushed off. The tissues on the table were rough when I wiped my nose on them, but I got all the tears off my face before steeling myself. I looked down at my clothes, seeing I had pajama pants and an oversized T-shirt on, so nothing was showing.

Just like everything else in life, I could do this, too.

I sucked in a deep breath and unlocked the door. I gripped the handle, and in a whoosh, Cade stood in front of me.

I met his concerned stare head-on, not giving a single inch. Sure, he could probably see the redness of my eyes, yet I didn't care.

"Baby." He stepped closer.

I took a step back, widening the door for them to come into the room. I couldn't let him touch me, not knowing what that touch would do right now. I needed distance.

Once the men were in the small space, it seemed almost claustrophobic, so I moved to the only window across the room as the door clicked shut.

Cade started toward me again.

"Don't," I warned him, my eyes growing intense.

He halted.

"Stay over there. Say what you need to say then get out."

He moved to the wall only a few feet to the side of me while Stiff and Boner stayed back by the door.

"Trixie, tell me what's in your head," he said.

I scoffed. "No. Say what you want and get out."

"Trixie …" he warned. "Why don't you trust me?" The words were pained as they came out, like I was physically hurting him.

"Oh, I don't know. Because fifteen years ago, you told me you weren't ever going to let me go, only to let me go in the most dick-ish way possible. Then you decided to lay a bomb on me that shakes the ground under my feet. So, no, Cade, I don't fucking trust you. And as far as you two go"—I aimed my stare at Boner and Stiff—"testing me isn't fucking happening. I've dealt with too many shitheads in my life. I'm done with that."

"I was a dick, and I told you why," Cade started.

"Then why even tell me all that shit? Because now, with our past Cade, I don't know if I could ever trust you. Especially after all of this."

Cade looked at Boner and Stiff then sighed. "Let's talk about trust for a minute. I'm gonna put even more trust in you. I'm going to tell you something that only three people know besides me. Boner, Stiff, and Bosco are the only ones. This shit's important, and I need to know I can count on you to keep it between us."

Oh, shit. My stomach did a somersault as I nodded.

"My father had me tailed that night we were together. The guy reported back to him that you were with me. My old man told me, if I didn't get my head in the game with his extra business, he'd make sure *you* paid. I played it off like you were just pussy to me. He didn't buy it."

My heart fell to the floor. Holy shit. Who would do that?

"That was the moment I knew I didn't have a choice other than to take him down. I made a plan and followed through. I got my club out of the business, had the Colonel begin his take over, and then shot my father."

I closed my eyes as my mind processed the barrage of words. He had shot his father? *He shot his father.* Holy fucking shit. My gut twisted in a knot so tight I didn't think it would ever release. He was right about one thing—this was huge. *This* was murder, and he trusted me with this information.

"Babe, I'm telling you the truth. I'm trusting you with this information because I believe in you ... in us," he said with such earnestness that my heart jumped.

"Trix," Boner said from across the room, and my eyes went to him. "He is. The only reason the club came on board with him telling you is because he loves you."

Cade whipped his head around to glare at Boner, and I felt my heart shatter. Damn, I was a moron. He didn't love me. That hurt.

"Spook, stop fucking around. Your woman is about ready to leave your ass. You don't throw all your cards on the table now, she's gone."

"It's too late." My chest hurt. I wanted them all to leave. "You said your peace; now, please, leave me alone."

Cade sliced his head back toward me, a new sense of determination coming off him. If I weren't holding up the wall with my back, I would have tried to move away. His breathing intensified, nostrils flared, and his eyes darkened, seeming to be working fast with thoughts behind them. Then he spoke, knocking me on my ass.

"He's right. Loved you fifteen years ago, love you now."

How many times in my life had I wished to hear those words coming from Cade's mouth? Now, here they were, and I couldn't take it anymore. I couldn't trust those words. What if all of this was another test to gauge me or something?

I shook my head. "Too late," I whispered.

He came to me quickly, pulling me into him.

I pushed at his chest. "Let go," I demanded.

"Trixie, I'm trying really hard here to be a patient man, but it's getting harder by the second. Me and my boys are the ones you can trust. Swear it on my fucking life."

I lost it. "Don't you know how fucking badly I want to believe you? Trust you? I'm back in your life for days, and you lay all this on the table! Tell me, Cade, if I can trust you to tell me the truth, did you help your father with his business?"

Cade stilled under me, and my stomach dropped, but I didn't let it show.

He shook his head as if he were clearing away some memories. His voice came out quiet, his eyes appearing pained. "Yeah, babe, I did. I don't wanna talk about the shit I did. Please don't make me," he pleaded. "I don't want that shit floating around in your head. I'm not that man. I'm the guy who was with you for six months. I'm the man who stands in front of you today. Everything in the past is exactly where it needs to stay."

"How do I get over that?" Because I had no clue. How did I live with the knowledge that he helped his father sell women, possibly even hurt them?

"I didn't have a choice, Trixie." He pulled me to him more firmly. "I had to follow what he said. He was too powerful not to. All you gotta do is believe in me, the man before you now."

For a flash, I saw the boy who had laid with me under the stars as I told him what each of the constellations were. I didn't think he cared about them, but he listened to my little freshman self.

I missed him. So damn much. My heart ached to the point of serious physical pain.

"I don't know if I can." My words were quiet and I hurt from the pained look on his face.

Tears sprang to my eyes, and I couldn't hide them.

"Try. For me, baby. You gotta try."

While I wanted to let him in, it was all too raw, too fresh.

Silence filled the space for long moments as my mind spun.

"I make no promises." I couldn't. My stubbornness wouldn't allow me to get walked all over again. However, I had that small glimmer of hope that he would prove himself to me. "If I find out you're lying to me about this, that you took advantage of my trust in any way, you'll never see me again, and I'll put a bullet in you myself."

The guys chuckled.

"Go," Cade barked out at the two guys.

I rested my head in the crook of his neck. He smelled of tobacco and Cade as I hugged him, wanting to be able to trust him. At that moment, however, I just needed comfort from my life, and I sought it in Cade's strong embrace.

TWELVE

SPOOK

I HELD TRIXIE TIGHT TO MY BODY AS SHE slept, both arms locked around her for fear she'd leave again. I wasn't going to let her go anywhere ever.

I'd been a fucking mess when I woke up to find her gone. Pissed didn't cut it. I almost punched Boner, Stiff, and Bosco. Then, when I couldn't find her for fucking hours and hours, I really lost it.

Dawg finally got a lock on her cell phone. That's how we found her at the hotel. I'd had to bribe the clerk to look up someone who only paid in cash. I knew she didn't use a card because I checked. I was pretty proud of her for that. She was pretty fucking smart when it came to not being found. That was good and bad.

I dropped hard information on her, not knowing what she'd do. Not that I thought for a second she'd go to the cops. No, that didn't cross my mind. My concern was for her. I wanted to be the one to hold her though all of this. Comfort her. Love her.

Boner being fucking right again, I needed to lay everything out on the table with her. I hoped it all didn't blow up in my face.

She moved her hand up and down my arm. Shit, I thought she was sleeping.

"I wanna talk to the Colonel."

"Don't think that's a good idea, Trixie." I kissed the back of her head, knowing despite my words, she would talk to him. She was too strong of a woman not to. "But, if you want to, I'm there with you."

Her head turned toward me. "Why?"

"Because he's not gonna be too happy that I told you."

She turned fully in my arms.

"Normally, the only people who know club business are in the club. This situation rides me differently. It happened so long ago, you're involved, and I want you as my woman, so I'm letting you in on it. When we struck the deal, it was under the assumption no one other than the club would know. Now you do, and I don't know how he's gonna take that." I included Trixie in the deal with the Colonel to be absolutely certain he wouldn't hurt her. I always wanted her protected, and that hadn't changed.

"I have to, Cade. I have to talk to him, find out if he's still doing it, if I can stop it." Her words came out fast. I had to stop her.

"One thing is a definite. You cannot get involved with that business. Ever."

She started again, and I squeezed her.

"Those fuckers don't play around, Trixie. You get involved with it, they'll try to take you away from me. That's not happening."

Just the thought of those fuckers getting their hands on her sent ice through my veins. I worked so damn hard to shield her from this life, not wanting any of it to touch her.

Her eyes lost a little of the determination. "I still feel like I need to talk to him. You have to understand that."

I did, but I didn't like it one bit.

"With me there."

"Fine. I'm still on the fence with you, though. I …" She shook her head into the pillow. "This is going to be hard for me."

"We'll work it out."

Done talking, I kissed her, and it only took moments for her body to give in. I had a raging hard-on, but I wouldn't push for sex. I just needed to kiss her so she'd know I wasn't full of shit. I needed to be connected to her in the simplest of ways.

It seemed like everything came full circle. My younger days were filled with want for her and my future. I couldn't have them both, so I gave up one for the other. Well, I'd be damned if I gave her up a second time.

I pulled away, looking deep into her eyes. "You're gonna trust me, Trixie. I'm gonna do everything in my damn power to make it happen."

"Could you just leave for a while?" Trixie asked from her desk in her office.

Although she said she had shit to catch up on, I wasn't quite ready to let her out of my sight yet. It'd been a day since I brought her home from the hotel, and I stayed on her the entire time or had one of my boys do it. Leaving her right now wasn't an option. Therefore, I put Boner in charge of the shop, having him filter things through me yet taking care of the day-to-day shit.

"Nah." I stretched out on the leather couch in the far corner of her office. "I'm comfortable."

"Whatever," she grumbled. "I'm not gonna run."

"I know." Because I'd be here so she wouldn't. I couldn't go through the hell of having her disappear again. No fucking way.

"Hovering over me is not going to win you any points in the trust department."

I sucked in deep. "Babe, I know. Just give me some time, and then shit'll go back to normal." Whatever in the fuck normal was. "Anyway, in a few hours, I have church at the clubhouse. I'll have to leave you here for a while." Damn if that didn't eat at my gut.

"I have Ike," she retorted.

"You mean the guy I took out?"

She shrugged. "He's been told to shoot first and ask questions later."

"Good." I'd still have one of my guys on her, too.

FOUR HOURS LATER, TRIXIE threw down her pen and yawned. "I'm gonna call him," she said just as I started to drift off. It snapped my attention to alert.

"I advise you don't." It was a long shot, but I rolled with it.

She picked up her cell, her hand slightly trembling as she pushed some buttons.

I sat up from the couch and ran my fingers through my hair. *Fucking hell.*

"It's Trixie … Can you come to my office tomorrow at three? … Because I need to talk to you … No, I can't. I have to work … Okay, then the next day? … Alright, at five. I'll be here." She swiped the phone off, leaning back in her chair with a heavy sigh.

"When?" I asked, even though I just heard.

"Two days. He'll be here at five."

"Alright." Fuck, I didn't want her to see that dick.

"You know, I always knew the Colonel was an asshole, but this"—she waved her hand in the air—"I just don't get. I mean, I don't get how anyone could do it. My father dealt in numbers. Numbers on the cards, money … not selling women." She shook her head. "At least, that's what I thought. Damn, I was a fool."

I moved to her, sitting on the edge of her desk. "You, Trixie, are anything but a fool. You were meant to stay clear of all of this business and would have …" I trailed off, not liking where my words were going.

"If I hadn't come to you about Nanette," she finished.

"Yeah."

"Why is that, Cade? If you felt this way about me, why did I have to come to you?"

I moved in front of her, and her legs spread, letting me in. "Because, Trixie, I'm no good for you. I'm an asshole who gets what he wants. I'm demanding as fuck in bed. My club is my soul. You deserve better than all this shit I'm throwing at you. I knew it then, and I know it now."

She tilted her head, but before she could say anything, I continued, "I'm a selfish bastard, though. As soon as I saw you back in my club, I knew I couldn't let you go a second time. That's why, plain and simple. You believe in fate?"

"I guess." Her eyes gleamed from the lights in the room, giving the green a shine.

"That's what this is. Fate stepping in, taking over, and I'm holding on."

She dropped her chin to her chest. Using my index finger, I lifted so she met my eyes.

"It's gonna be okay." I'd damn well do anything and everything I could to make sure of that.

AFTER HAVING A CONVERSATION with Ike about staying close to Trixie, I rushed to the club. I was going to be fucking late, something I didn't do.

It was time to give Fox his money, and I needed to get a vote on it before I handed it over. Fuck, it was my mom, and I felt like an asshole, but Fox could cause us some serious trouble. I didn't need that shit. I'd told Mom to stay away from his table, but she hadn't listened.

I entered the clubhouse to find the guys standing around.

"About time," Bosco chided.

"Got held up. Let's start." I tossed my phone on the table outside the door before entering the room.

The smell of smoke and years of decisions billowed through the air. Our symbol—the skull with Vipers on either side of it—was painted on the far wall. The other had pictures of good times we'd had in the club. In the center sat three large, square tables that we pushed together to make one long table with padded chairs around it.

I took my seat at the head as the guys piled in. Boner sat to my left, Stiff to my right, and Dawg next to him with everyone else sitting scattered.

I slammed the gavel down, and we went through all the shit with the garage and numbers first. Most of that was to the point.

"One more vote we need to do." I looked around the table, meeting each man head-on. "My mother is four k in the hole with Fox. He knows she doesn't have that kind of money and would come to me for it. If I pay it, we're on his radar, and when it happens again, we'll be expected to pay. If I don't pay, he puts my mom out on the streets to work it off." I shook my head. "We need to vote if I should give her the money." Fuck, I hated this, hated she put me in this position.

"All those in favor of me giving her the money, say yes and raise your hand." Everyone's hand in the room flew up. Every. Single. Fucking. One.

I looked down at the table. My brothers were going to take this full-out, head-on if it came to that. Hopefully, my mother would get her shit together, though.

"Vote is yes. Approved."

"We gotta talk about the Colonel and Trixie," Bosco said, cracking his big knuckles. "What's going on with that?"

"She and I are meeting with him in a couple of days." Nothing more needed to be said, because I didn't have anything else to give them.

He nodded.

I slammed the gavel back down. "Adjourned."

THIRTEEN

SPOOK

"I KNEW YOU'D COME THROUGH FOR ME," my mother cheered when I picked her up the next day to go pay off her debts. I could have given her the money and let her pay it, but Fox knew it was from me in the first place, so I might as well cut it off at the head. Also, I couldn't trust my mother to actually pay it instead of betting again and losing.

"Last fucking time, Mom. I mean it, too. You gotta get a job selling your ass to pay back your debt, you're doing it. You don't start thinking smart, you're gonna piss off the club, and we'll cut you off altogether." I stared out the window, but in my peripheral vision, I saw her mouth drop.

"You don't mean that. My boys wouldn't turn their backs on me."

"Your boys are sick of your shit. You have enough to live on and be comfortable. Stay off the fucking tables. Do you understand?"

I was fucking done.

We pulled up to Fox's estate. It didn't surprise me one bit that he had a gate.

I hit the buzzer, and a flowery female voice came over the line. "Yes?"

"Spook and Larraine here to see Fox."

"Hang on one moment." She was gone for a good five minutes before she came back on. "You may come in, but it is advised you leave all weapons in the car as you will be searched upon entrance."

"Got it." I'd already put my Glock in the glove box. I wasn't fucking stupid. We had his money; therefore, he had no reason to hurt either one of us.

The drive was lined with trees on each side while we drove on concrete. The home came into view. I was used to big things, considering our compound, but this brought overindulgence to a whole new level.

Yellow? The whole three-story, windows everywhere house had stucco tinted in yellow. Well, wasn't this happy and cheery.

The main door opened as I put the car in park. A man in a black suit, white shirt, and black tie stepped out, walking with purpose toward the car.

I got out, raising my hands in the air as he came to me. Not saying a word, he patted me down, finding nothing. He did the same to my mother, even looking in her purse and pulling out the large envelope with the money in it.

"Money," she said.

He grunted, opened it to assess that we weren't lying, and then finally gave it back to her.

"This way." He took off, walking up the massive staircase.

We followed.

To say the house was overdone would be an understatement. Holy fuck. Art lined the walls of the foyer with a huge sculpture in the center of it. The whole thing screamed gaudy as fuck. Plus, there were so many twists and turns I couldn't tell where the hell we were going.

"Follow," the big brute ordered.

I wasn't a man used to taking orders, so him giving them to me gave me more fuel to be pissed at my mother.

The guy opened a door. "In."

We stepped into a fucking huge-ass office. It was nothing like either of the two I had. Bookshelves lined two of the walls from floor to ceiling, which had to be more than ten feet tall, with a ladder propped up to the side. The monstrosity of a desk took up half a room with the computer on top, looking like a kid's toy.

The door reopened, and Fox stepped through. He was in his fifties with silver hair and a cleanly shaven face. He had on a pure white suit, including his shoes. He was drying his hands on a paper towel, his eyes cold.

"I trust you have my money?" he asked, moving to the chair and taking a seat. He held out his arm, motioning to the two seats in front of him.

"Yes, Mr. Fox," my mother said, reaching into her purse.

"So, why do I have the honor of you being here, Spook?" He chuckled at my name, not that I gave a fuck.

"You knew it would be coming from me, so I'm here."

My mother rose, handing him the envelope, then sat back down.

"Now she's clear. She doesn't sit at any more of your tables, Fox."

"Ah, so you came to issue orders, did ya?" He rubbed his chin with his polished hand like he was thinking. "How about this: your mother keeps herself away from my tables, and there's no problems? If she comes back, then we all have problems."

I nodded. It was fair. I'd have to figure out how to put my mother on a fucking leash.

He smacked his hands together. "See? I get my money, and everyone is happy." He gave a smile that said he knew he'd be seeing me again. Fucker.

I stood up. "We're going."

My mother followed suit.

"Yes, and I'll see you soon, Larraine." He winked, and my fire burned hot. If my fucking mother went back, I'd kill her my own goddamned self.

I NODDED TO IKE AS I WALKED into Trixie's office, carrying Italian for lunch.

After reaming my mother in the car, I picked up my favorite food before heading to Sirens. I needed to get my mother and her shit out of my head, and Trixie was just the person to do it.

"Back already?" she asked, taking off those sexy as fuck glasses and tossing them to the desk. Her hair was a mess on top of her head, but she looked fucking hot. "I mean, you weren't supposed to be here until four."

I held up the bags. "Brought you lunch."

She gave me the sexiest smirk. "You think feeding me is gonna get you in my good graces?"

I shrugged, putting the food on her desk. "Whatever works."

She cleared off her desk then pulled the food out of the paper bag while I pulled a chair up and opened the containers.

"Lasagna, bread, and salad," I told her as she sniffed the air.

"God, it smells so good." She took her first bite and moaned. "I love Bastas."

I said nothing. I simply watched her eat with vigor. The fork gliding in and out of her mouth made my cock hard as a brick. I shook my head and began eating.

"So, Trixie, it's a little late for this, but tell me about yourself."

She laughed. "Now you ask me this?" She rolled her eyes before taking another bite of bread. "There's not much to tell, Cade. I work. Sirens is my life. The Colonel isn't in my life much. That's it." She waved her fork in the air then paused, shock hitting her face.

"What?"

"The Colonel paid for my college. He used the money from the girls to pay for it." Her wide eyes looked lost.

"Trixie, it's over and done with now. You can't put that shit on your shoulders." The money might have come from a dubious source, but none of that mattered now. It was a thing of the past, and she needed to lock it away as that.

She didn't say anything, just stared.

"Trixie?"

Her eyes came to me. "Sorry. I can't help feeling dirty about it."

I knew the feeling all too well.

"Sometimes, this kind of dirt doesn't wash off," I admitted.

"Ever?"

"Ever. It stays with ya, but you learn to live with it and move on."

She set down her fork, worry playing in her eyes. "I'm nervous about seeing him, knowing now what he does. I hate it."

"I know, but that's his shit, and you do not get involved with it," I repeated.

"I get that. That doesn't mean I have to like any of this."

"No, you don't. But you deal and move on." I felt the rock hit my gut. "Or try to."

She went back to eating her food. "I went to college and got a degree in business. I didn't do the partying thing. I mostly kept to myself. I didn't want to go, but my father demanded it, so I did. When I graduated, no one came to the ceremony." She looked down in despair.

I got up, moving to her. I picked her up from the chair as she let out a small yelp. Then I sat down on the couch with her in my lap. She felt perfect there.

"What the hell?"

"Keep going. Can't have you talking about this shit without being close to ya. I'm sorry you didn't have anyone there." Damn, that shit hurt, but I had no doubt that it made her a stronger woman.

"Yeah. After that, I tried a few of the local offices, and it wasn't my thing. Then this place came up for sale, so I got a loan and bought it." She laid back against me. "And that brings us to now."

"Do you still like to color in those books?"

Her breath hitched. "You remember."

She used to have these weird books that had different things in them, like stars and moons. She'd use these gel pen things to color, saying it calmed her.

"I haven't done that in a really long time. What about you? Do you still work on bikes?"

I sighed. "No. I miss it, though. I work more in the office now. Some days, I just wanna pick up a wrench and get to work."

She turned to me. "Then do it. What's stopping you?"

"There's always something that has to be done."

She rested her hand on mine that was on her knee. "You used to talk about all the different parts of a bike, how to do this and that to them. I had no clue what the hell you were talking about, but you were so excited about it, which made me excited for you."

"Yeah, shit happens." Fuck, life happens.

"You've gotta do what makes you happy. We only get one life; we have to do what we can to stay sane." She laughed.

"What do you do?"

"I work." She looked around her office. "That's it."

"Sounds like you need to get out more. Maybe poker at the clubhouse."

She scowled at me. "What, for another test?"

"Easy there, wildcat. Just for fun."

She shook her head as a knock sounded on the door. She tried to pull off my lap, but I didn't release her.

"Yeah," I called out, which got me another glare.

"Ike."

"Come in."

"Let me go and stop giving my staff orders, or I'll cut off your fucking balls. You need to know this right now; this is my club. Mine. I don't tell you how to run your club, so you don't tell me how to run mine."

I pulled her down for a quick kiss that she wasn't expecting then turned toward the door.

"Yeah," I said as Trixie turned around, still in my arms.

"What's going on, Ike?" she asked.

"Nanette. Can't find her anywhere. Checked phone, credit cards, relatives—I got nothing. None of my contacts have spotted her since that night at Vipers Creed. She's hunkered down deep."

"Fuck." Trixie pulled away from me, and I released her this time. "Alright, keep on it. She's gotta be here somewhere."

When Ike left the room, Trixie paced, chewing her nail.

"She must be with a boyfriend or something."

"Don't know, but baby, I'm tellin' ya, you ain't gettin' your money back."

She growled—yes, growled. "Watch me."

I laughed, loving how feisty and determined she when she wanted something. Now I just needed to get that determination on me.

FOURTEEN

TRIX

"**H**ERE'S THE BOOZE ORDER AND THE schedule for the girls for the next two weeks," Jett said, standing at my desk. She'd had a lot thrown on her shoulders these past few days and handled it like a pro.

I took the papers. "Thank you for taking on all this shit."

She shrugged. "I've got your back." Yeah, she did.

"I know. What all needs to be taken care of?"

Her smirk told me I wouldn't like what she had to give me.

She held out a file folder. "Expense reports for this month."

I huffed out a laugh. "Yay, fun for me."

"I can go over them if you like."

I waved her off. "No, I'll do it. I'll make sure all the numbers add up."

Her eyes drifted behind me to the man currently lying on my couch. It was my turn to silently shrug.

"You good?"

I nodded. "Yeah. I'm good." Not really, but Sirens was the only stable thing I had going right now.

"Alright, I've got things to do," she said, giving me a slight wave before heading out the door.

"You like doing all this shit?" Cade asked from the couch as soon as Jett left.

I thought he was asleep, considering I hadn't heard much from him, but looking over at him, I saw he was typing on his phone, calm as could be. Not me, I was a nervous wreck. The Colonel would be here soon.

"What?" I asked stupidly, putting the papers in my hand down on the desk.

He waved his hand in the air, motioning to my desk. "The paperwork. Do you enjoy it all?"

I tilted my head, taking him in. I popped my lips and answered honestly. "*Like doing* isn't what I would call it. I look at it as, if I want Sirens to be run right, I need to have my hands in everything. It's the only way I know for sure what's going on all the time."

He chuckled, and I lifted a brow. Surely, he wasn't laughing at me.

He shook his head. "No, not laughing at you. I'm laughing at us."

"And why would that be?"

He licked his sexy bottom lip, and I felt my belly quiver. "You and I, we're cut from the same cloth."

When he didn't continue, I asked, "And that means …?"

"I run the garage and the club. I'm neck deep in paperwork all the time. After my dad made a fucking mess out of everything, I took it all on my shoulders."

A warm feeling spread through my chest, yet something puzzled me. "But you've been spending tons of time with me here. I haven't seen you do a single piece of paperwork in that time." Hell, since three days ago when he took me out of the hotel, he'd been with me almost nonstop.

He held up his phone, shaking it from side to side. "Boner was on my ass about not delegating, so I did. He's been scanning the important shit to my email and handling the rest. This way, I'm still taking care of shit and doing what I need to get done."

"You've put all this in motion in the last few days?"

His laughter slithered down my spine. I'd always loved it.

"Yeah. We move quickly when it's important."

"You know you don't have to be here all afternoon," I quipped.

He leaned forward, his elbows on his knees, and laced his fingers together. "Trixie, the only way I'm gonna get you to trust me is if I'm here. You know all my shit now …" He trailed off.

"How do you trust that I won't go to the cops or something?" Not that I ever would, not in a million years.

He rose, coming at me. I turned my chair on its swivel as he dropped to his knees in front of me, his eyes alight with lust and caring. The action hit me hard. It was profound in a way I couldn't explain.

He grabbed my hands, and the warmth from his touch had my eyes going to our connection. "Fifteen years ago, you tunneled your way into my heart." He cleared his throat. "One look at you in my clubhouse, and that was all it took. I knew … *knew* you were mine. In knowing this down to my fucking bones, I trust you completely. I know I have to earn yours. I get it, and I'm doing it by spending time with you, fucking you, and dealing with the hard shit like talking to the Colonel. When I have shit that's really important, like a meeting with the boys, then I deal and come back to you. I'll always come back to you … for you."

Tears welled in my eyes, and I tried with super human strength to push them back.

I leaned over and wrapped my arms around his neck, pulling him to me, my face burrowing in his neck. I wanted to believe it. I did. However, I was scared. Terrified.

His words wouldn't normally cut me, but those … Those cut me to the quick, and I latched on to every single one of them as I held him tight.

We stayed in that position for long moments before lifting our heads. When we did, he kissed me, sexy and sultry and with as much passion as ever, but it was also slow and sweet. He cupped my cheeks as he surprised me with the type of kiss and then pulled away.

"You get me now, Trixie?"

I nodded because I did, even if everything was a mess right now.

"Good." He kissed my forehead. "What about me killing my father?"

The air left my sails. Even after having time to process it, it still seemed so surreal, but it was now my reality. I understood why Cade had done what he did. While murder was a horrible thing, I didn't feel outrage or even fear from him. If anything, it made me realize the lengths Cade would go to for me.

I looked into his captivating eyes. "Cade, I'm not saying that I'm alright with you killing people, but I get why you had to take out your father."

"Does it scare you?" he asked hesitantly.

I bent over and touched my lips to his. "No." I stared into his eyes. I couldn't give him exactly what he needed at the moment, but I hoped my eyes told him what he needed to know.

"Good, Trixie, good." He kissed me hard then rose. "Your dad should be here in an hour."

I looked at the clock, and a boulder fell in my gut. One hour. *Shit*.

Cade moved back to the couch and sat down, pulling out his phone and getting back to work. I turned back to my desk, mentally preparing myself for the meeting with my father.

I wasn't going to lie. I was happy Cade was here. My father had always made me nervous growing up. I'd always felt more like an obligation to him than a daughter. I learned quickly how to take care of myself, because my father hadn't cared if I had eaten or bathed, and the nannies always did the bare minimum. He always told me that I *"needed to grow up,"* which I did faster than any child should. Regardless, I survived and grew out of it, becoming tougher than most women.

The boulder in my stomach flipped and flopped, making me queasy. It felt like forever before there was a knock on the door, and Jett popped her head inside, her face pale as a ghost. I knew the Colonel was here.

Jett had never liked him, told me he freaked her way the hell out. She had a right to be seriously scared.

"The Colonel's here," she said softly, her eyes moving to Cade.

"Let him in," I said and mouthed, *"It's okay,"* and she nodded, shutting the door.

Cade pulled a chair around from the front of the desk and sat next to me, cool and calm. I wish I had that, but no, my heart was pumping so fast I was surprised my body didn't spasm. Hopefully, it didn't show on the outside.

The door opened, and in stepped my father, the Colonel. The air seemed to get sucked out of the room as his eyes came to mine. He looked as good as always in black slacks with a pressed crease down the middle and a white shirt unbuttoned at the collar. His shoes were the expensive Italian kind.

His face was worn yet firm. He had lines by his eyes, which I knew didn't come from laughing. I'd had yet to ever hear him laugh. They had to be from all the scowls. My same green eyes locked on me then swung to Cade.

"Well, this is interesting," he said in a low tone as he shut the door behind him and walked into the space like he owned it.

I wouldn't show weakness, not ever. As much as I wanted to either pace or move my leg up and down, I did neither. I was stoic, even clasping my hands together so I didn't start scratching the desk. If I did that, then he'd know I was nervous.

"Hi, Colonel. Please, have a seat." I gestured to the chair in front of me.

"You packing?" Cade asked from beside me.

"Always. You?" he countered.

Cade nodded. I had mine, too, under the desk, but it was nice to know everyone was at play here. Anything was possible with the Colonel.

My father sat, crossing one ankle over his knee and sitting back in the chair, relaxed as can be.

"You summoned me," he quipped.

My heart rate sped up, and I tried to slow it, but it was on a warpath. I wanted to ask the question yet stumbled on it, my normal bravado taking a back seat when I needed it the most.

"I told her about the girls," Cade said, shocking me. One, for bailing me out. Two, because I wanted to kiss him for having the balls to flat out say it. I wanted some of those balls when it came to the man sitting before me.

The Colonel remained stoic. "And what girls would this be?"

Cade stiffened beside me while I kept my eyes trained on my father.

"I told her about my father's side business that you took over."

The Colonel's eyes sliced to Cade as some unknown to me conversation went through them. I wanted to be in one of their heads.

"I have no idea what you're talking about," he claimed, and my heart dropped.

While I hadn't really expected him to tell me, part of me had hoped. That little girl inside who had always wanted her father's approval wanted to think he'd tell me the truth. I knew better, yet I wished he would have turned over a new leaf. I let the hope die along with everything I had always wanted for in a father.

"The business you took over for Spook's father," I finally spoke. "Why would you do this?"

Nothing on his face gave him away. He wasn't going to tell us anything.

"Cade's putting some serious ideas in your head. Lies, lies, lies. You trying to get in my daughter's pants again?" he accused.

"Just finish this, Colonel. She knows. Deal with it," Cade retorted in a clipped tone.

My father looked me straight in the eye, the intensity coming off him in waves. "You're going to believe him? Come on, Trix; you're smarter than that," he scoffed like it was all the same to him. He really didn't give a shit if I believed him or not.

"Why would Spook lie?"

My father shrugged. "Who the fuck knows?"

"I'm not fucking lying," Cade growled.

My father stared at Cade, and I could feel the anger billowing off the man beside me.

"First, why would anyone admit to anything of the sort? That would be a fool's move, and I am no fool. Second, if someone were to know such damaging information, they would have to be dealt with." The last words were snapped tight.

Coldness took over my body. It was a threat to me.

My throat clogged, and I couldn't speak. It shouldn't be a surprise, considering everything I'd learned, but not once in my life had he ever threatened to *deal* with me. Never once laid a hand on me. He'd gone and done it now. I was officially petrified of the man.

"You come fucking near her, and I'll kill you," Cade fumed, his body still relaxed, but not his temper.

Cade was right; this was a bad idea. I was smarter than this and should have played the outcome in my head better, not letting all the new information clog me up. That was on me.

When I reached over and put my hand on Cade's knee, his hand came to the top of mine and squeezed. I needed it, needed the reassurance, his comfort.

"I won't say anything." My words came out so much smaller than I wanted, allowing the bit of hurt to come through, which was a mistake. The Colonel would use it. I kicked myself for not having the control.

"I know you won't say a word because you have no proof of anything. I, on the other hand, do." He paused, his eyes going to Cade. "Proof that your boy here killed his father in cold blood. I'd hate for that information to get into the wrong hands." His face was so still. Nothing, not a tick or an eye movement, to tell me he was lying.

Cade was wrong. Someone else knew. *Shit.*

"You asshole," Cade ground out.

This time, my father gave a devilish smirk. "Never play all your cards. You never know when you'll need one in reserve," he said to both of us.

Shit, his teachings came back to me. He'd always told me that, if there were a way to hold a card back to use at a later time, do it.

His eyes were cold, so cold the frost filled my veins. "I'm done." He stood and went to the door. I went to say something, but he turned back to me. "Watch yourself," he said, slamming the door behind him.

Holy shit. I allowed my body to shake because it so desperately needed it. I'd held it all in, and if I didn't let it out, I was going to implode.

Cade must have seen it, because he pulled me out of the chair and plopped me in his lap. He rubbed my arms and kissed the top of my head, not saying anything. I clung to his warmth, allowing him to chip off the ice I felt to my bones. I needed the quiet to process everything that happened. I felt like my life was in a blender that was turned on high. A chill ran up my back.

"Trixie, we're leaving here and going to your place. I want you to pack everything you need for a while. You're coming to stay with me. If you're here and I'm not, I'm gonna have a man on you. I don't know what the fuck he's thinking, but I'm not taking any chances."

I burrowed farther into him. Cade wanted to take care of me, protect me. I'd been protecting myself for so damn long it felt nice to have someone help with the burden. I felt a small part of me crack.

Thoughts of all my options played in my head: Go back home alone? No thank you. Stay with Ike or Jett? Nope, not bringing the Colonel down on them.

I had to start somewhere with Cade, and he'd already started building the blocks of trust by protecting and trusting me. If I stayed with him, then I'd let the cards fall where they may.

"Okay."

"You're not gonna fight me on this?" he questioned.

"No." My voice lowered to a whisper. "I'm scared, and you make me feel safe."

He kissed my head again and chuckled. "And here I thought you were gonna be a challenge."

"I'll always be a challenge." I would be, but when it came to him protecting me, the trust was building.

FIFTEEN

TRIX

CADE WAS ON THE PHONE WHILE I finished up my work. After, we went home to pack my clothes. He was sweet, checking out the house before letting me in and then carrying my bags out to my car for me. I drove it while he followed on his bike right behind me.

We finally arrived at the compound around eleven. It was still early for me, but I was wiped. These last few days had been a whirlwind of activity with information, and I was still reeling.

Cade directed me to one of the cement-block buildings off to the side of the main clubhouse. It was fairly big, but the outside was stark. It didn't have the plants that some of the others had, and when he opened the door, I could see why. The place was a pit. There were clothes every which way, empty pizza boxes. It was nothing like Cade's office or his room at the club that were both organized and put together.

The wide space had two couches, a recliner, and a large coffee table in the center with a mammoth seventy-three-inch television hanging on the wall. All of it was covered in clothes, empty containers. Basically, it was a complete disaster.

"Welcome," he said as if I didn't need a hazmat suit.

"Really, Cade?"

He shrugged. "It's home. Only people who come in here are me and sometimes my mom."

"And let me guess, your mother cleans it up for ya."

He smiled huge. "It's been a while."

"Momma's boy," I teased, kicking some clothes out of my path.

He laughed, dropping my bags on the floor. He immediately started picking up the clothes, throwing them in a huge pile in the corner of the room. Just doing that, I could now see the beige carpet. At least the place didn't stink.

"Want something to drink?" he offered, walking into his surprisingly modern kitchen. It had stainless steel appliances and a dark granite-type countertop that was littered in shit. He grabbed a large, black garbage bag; did an arm swipe and pushed everything into it.

"Interesting way to clean," I commented, moving farther into the space.

"Gotta do what I gotta do," he quipped, picking up my bags then moving down a hallway. I followed.

When we got to his bedroom, I was shocked. It was nothing like the rest of the house. No, this room was pretty clean except the messy bed, but who made their beds anymore?

My mind reeled to Stacy the night I was here for the party.

"Do I need to fumigate the sheets?" I asked, not liking this. I thought about the clubhouse bed. Shit, I should have fumigated those.

"Told you, no one's been in here but me."

"And the clubhouse?" Why did I ask that? Why, why, why? I didn't want to know the answer, yet I opened my big damned mouth.

"You really wanna know? Because I'll tell ya flat-out, Trixie. I'm not gonna keep shit from you, but you've gotta really want the answers to the questions you ask."

I thought for a bit and chewed on my bottom lip. I already knew the answer, and I didn't need to hear it.

"I'm not sleeping in the clubhouse."

He chuckled. "Babe, I'll buy a new fucking bed. New everything." He flipped on the lights to the en suite bathroom, which was also fairly decent. "Gotta say, I love your fire, babe."

He dropped my bags and pulled me flush with his body. I was so damn tired from the day, but his touch sparked the flame inside me.

He kissed me, hard and deep. I needed this, needed to feel alive. I needed him to wash all of the shit from the day away. I needed my head on something else besides the mess that my life had turned into. I had Nanette owing me a chunk of change, my father was a lying piece of shit, and I was mixed up with Cade and didn't know if I could trust it.

He wrapped his hand in my hair, turning my head to go deeper into my mouth. I loved when he took control. The taste of Cade burst across my tongue, and wetness coated me.

He wasted no time, somehow unbuttoning my jeans and getting them and my thong off without breaking the kiss. I had to release and break the kiss when he ripped my shirt over my head then did the same to himself. This wasn't sweet and slow. No, this was fast and demanding.

"Need to fuck you hard," he growled, his words burning me.

"God, yes."

He gave me another brutal kiss then turned me around and pushed me on the bed. My chest hit the cold sheets. I heard the thump of his buckle hitting the floor and the rustle of clothes. The bed dipped, and without words, he positioned my knees under me then slammed inside. I put my face in the sheets and screamed, the burn and pleasure mingled together in a rainbow of colors.

His thrusts shook the bed, and I clawed at the sheets as he drove me higher and higher. A slap came to my ass, and I turned to him.

"That's for not believing me."

He gave me more slaps to my ass, so many I lost count, but he was fucking me so damn good that the fire it caused only made me hotter.

"You know I'll always protect you?"

When I didn't answer, he slapped my mound, and heat cascaded all the way up to my core.

"Answer me," he demanded.

"Yes …" I said shakily.

He smiled predatorily and began pumping into me harder.

I gasped, feeling like this orgasm was going to be bigger than ever. Stars sparked in my eyes as the pleasure hit. However, he didn't lessen his pace, just continued to make me climb higher and higher. I didn't know if I had several orgasms in a row or if it was only a long one that never stopped.

He groaned, and then his weight fell on top of me, his face going to my neck. He nuzzled me, inhaling me. Every single time he did this, my heart tripped over itself. His weight felt nice, safe, comforting.

He rolled off, cleaning up while I did the same. When we climbed into bed, he pulled my back to his front, and I snuggled into him willingly. He wrapped his arms around me tight, and I passed out within seconds.

IN THE MIDDLE OF THE NIGHT, I was rolled onto my back, and I opened my eyes groggily. Cade brushed his hands up and down my legs as he sat between them.

"What's going on?" I asked, seeing his eyes full of lust, making my clit wake up.

He continued to rub up and down my legs, my naked body on full display to him.

"I wanna show you something."

With my brow raised, I asked, "In the middle of the night?"

He reached over to the side of the bed, pulling out a belt. To say I was shocked was an understatement.

"What do you need a belt for?"

A sexy grin came across his lips, and I had the urge to sit up and lick them.

"You're starting to trust me?"

I nodded because it was true.

"I wanna show you pleasure, Trixie."

"With what?" Surely, he wasn't going to slap me with it. *That* wasn't happening.

"Tying you to my bed."

"No," was my knee-jerk response. I couldn't be trapped with no way of getting out.

I moved to get up, but Cade's body came down on mine, pinning me to the bed. His thighs on mine didn't allow any of my skin to be without him. I felt caged in, trapped, and my flight response hit me hard.

"Trixie." His voice was soft, which caught me off guard.

I looked up into his eyes. Sparks were in them, but not angry ones … lustful ones.

"Off!" I could hear the panic in my tone, but he didn't move.

"Would I ever hurt you?"

My mind reeled. Physically, no. Emotionally, he'd done it once, so why wouldn't he do it again?

"No," I told him, fully believing he would do anything in his power to make sure nothing hurt me …physically. I even believed he'd lay his life down for me if he had to.

"Right." He brushed his lips against mine in the softest, featherlike kiss, dousing some of the flames of my anger. "I wanna make you feel good. I wanna show you that even with your arms tied above your head, you're safe with me. That you can fully trust me."

I shook my head. "I can't."

He brushed his lips over mine again. "I told you I would do anything to earn your trust, Trixie." He kissed the tip of my nose. "Anything. Trust me to take care of you."

Being helpless was something that I'd worked my entire life at not being. I didn't want to put that trust into someone who would crush me underneath their feet. This was bigger than just letting Cade in, trusting him. This was letting him fully into my heart, too. I just knew this would break everything down and push everything away. Every wall I had would crumble, and I didn't know if I could do that.

I would never tell him this, of course, but my heart was already feeling the punch.

"Please," he said softly.

I could feel the tears prick the backs of my eyes. He wanted this, and as scared as I was, I could do it.

"Alright, but if I want the belt off, you'll take it off?"

"I promise you won't want it off."

"Cade," I warned. I was on the edge. If I couldn't have his word, I was backing down.

"I promise."

I let out a deep sigh as he rose from my body.

Reaching up to the slotted headboard, I wrapped my hands around it. I could feel the small tremors through my fingertips as I breathed in and out slowly.

"I'll take care of you," he said, climbing up the bed and fastening the leather around my wrists, tying them to the bed. I gave a tug, but they didn't budge.

I kept breathing as the panic rose even higher. I talked myself down. *I can do this.*

He moved down the bed, a devilish smile on his face. "Damn, you are so fucking sexy, babe."

I said nothing. My body felt wound tight, and it was taking everything I had to stay rooted to the bed.

"I want you to lie back and relax, Trixie. Trust that I'll make you feel good. Trust that I'd never devalue that trust once you give it to me. I'll never make the same mistake I did when I was a kid."

His eyes pleaded with me, so I closed mine then slowly opened them. My nerves were flying all over the place, and I couldn't get them to calm down, to settle and let this happen.

"That's it, baby," he coaxed, leaning up to my ear. The sexy, deep rumble mixed with his smell intoxicated me, helping my nerves settle even further.

He kissed my ear, neck, jaw, shoulder blades, and lavished attention on my nipples. As he sucked, I pressed my body up into him. The way he gave me the hot heat of his mouth, followed by intense sucking, felt so damn good. Each movement floated to my core.

I yanked on the belt, wanting to put my hands in his hair, but I came up very short. It was frustrating yet a small bit liberating, as well. Cade was taking care of me, and damn, did it feel so good.

The panic began to recede. I stopped and enjoyed the feel of his tongue moving down my body, circling my belly button and moving to the top of my mound. He placed kisses there. It was nice, but I needed him lower.

I raised my hips, trying to get his mouth right where I needed him, but all it got me was a heavy arm across my hips, holding me down.

Moans and whimpers were coming from deep in my throat. My body was an electric wire, ready to ignite and detonate. One long, slow lick from my ass to my clit had me whimpering.

"Fuck, you taste so damn good, Trixie. This is my pussy."

I said nothing, my eyes rolling into the back of my head with pleasure.

A slap to my thigh had my head popping up. His eyes were intensely focused on me.

"Mine, right, Trixie?"

I groaned as the heat from the hit made me needier.

"Answer me," he demanded.

I didn't want to tell him it was his pussy, but I needed him to help me release. The buildup was too much.

"Yes," I whispered softly.

"Damn fucking right. Now I'm gonna eat *my* pussy." And he did. God, did he.

Flicks of his tongue, fast then slow, hard then feather light, sent me so damn close to the edge. His teeth nipped, making me jump as he darted his tongue inside of me deep. Once he inserted his finger, finding that most sensitive spot inside my core, and sucked on my clit hard, I came. And I was right. I was a ticking time bomb that exploded into another orbit. I was floating on a high so big, so huge I never wanted to come down.

I felt him at my pussy, sucking and licking all of my release as I started to come down. My mind wanted to chase that euphoric high, but I couldn't.

"Now my cock," he demanded, wrapping himself and rising over me.

He pushed into me hard, and air caught in my throat. It felt so damn good, so right. His lips touched mine, and I could taste myself on him. That, too, felt right. Me mixed with him. Damn.

This time, Cade went slow, gentle, and dare I say, lovingly with each of his strokes. He kept his elbows on either side of my neck with his hands in my hair.

"Look at me," he whispered, and when I did, tears pricked at the backs of my eyes as I felt my heart begin to thump hard for the boy who had taken it so long ago.

I wished I could wrap my arms around him, but instead, I wrapped my legs, needing him everywhere on me.

The slow burn began building and building. With each thrust of his hips and the gaze in his eyes, I was lost in Cade. Lost in us. Each moment that ticked by was another inch closer I felt to Cade until I couldn't get any closer ... until I felt it coming, and my muscles contracted.

"That's it, baby. I'm coming with you."

That was it. We both came together in a crescendo of emotions wrapped in one orgasm. It was so much bigger than I'd even thought it could be. No, it wasn't a screaming orgasm; it was loving, unconditional and everything I'd always wanted from a man, from *this* man.

His head fell to my neck where he inhaled me, and I lost the battle with the tears. It was only one, but I needed it. This was the most intimate feeling, intimate act, that I'd ever experienced with another human being in my life, and it scared the ever-loving shit out me.

SIXTEEN

SPOOK

TRIXIE TRIED TO WALK IN FRONT OF ME, but I grabbed her, lacing my fingers in hers. She sighed and slowed her pace to mine. She'd been off since we woke in my bed about an hour ago, but I'd expected her to be. Hell, I was proud of her for working through all she'd learned.

When that motherfucker threatened her, it took everything I had not to pull out my gun and shoot him dead on sight. The one—*the only*—damn reason I didn't was because Trixie didn't need to see that shit. I was trying to build her fucking trust, not have her screaming and running away from me.

She may not admit it, but a part of her cared for her father. He was the only family she had. It was my fucking ambition to make sure she felt like she had family with me and my club, and it felt good that I could do that for her.

The thing was, it wasn't going to be hard. The boys already liked her, approved of her. She had yet to actually meet one of the very few ol' ladies. I would have to change that fast because not only was I going to give her a family, but I was giving her the club—my life. But one thing at a time.

I didn't normally eat much at my place unless it was takeout, and she needed food. Therefore, I opened the clubhouse door where the lights were blazing, but the room was fairly quiet. Two of the mouses were scurrying around, cleaning up the beer bottles and shit off the floors. They had barely anything on.

I knew the instant Trixie saw them, because she stilled next to me.

I wrapped my arm around her. "Baby, a few of the girls stay in a room in the basement." To this, she jolted more. Shit. "It's part of the club. The girls stay here, and we provide them protection."

"And they fuck you." Her voice was a tone that communicated she did not like this idea one little bit. I had to admit, I fucking liked that shit.

"They fuck the guys. Not me." I pulled her close so her eyes were connected with mine. "Only *you* get to fuck me."

She rolled her eyes like she didn't believe me, but I was dead serious.

In a quiet tone, she asked, "What if you get bored in six months or a year or …" Her fire was there, but it was laced with a hint of sadness.

I brushed my lips against hers so softly it was a whisper. Damn, she smelled good. "Never. You're all I need, babe."

Her eyes went lazy, and I loved that my words did that shit to her. She wanted to believe, and that was enough for me right now. It would take me time, and I fucking sucked at being patient, but for Trixie, I'd do anything.

"Let me feed you."

She gave a slight nod, and I pulled her toward the kitchen area of the club. It was a large room that the Army had used as a mess hall. We had tables and chairs lined around with some of the brothers up toward the front where the food was.

Our club was different than a lot around. All the brothers lived on the compound in one of the outbuildings. We didn't have places out in the city. No, we were a family who lived, worked, and breathed together. Somehow, it all worked.

"Seriously, they cook your food, too?" Trixie questioned, noticing the mouses running around, putting eggs, bacon, and the like on the buffet.

I chuckled. "Gotta earn their keep."

We walked up to the table loaded with brothers.

"Well, well, well, he's already got ya moved in, Trixie?" Boner asked with a huge smile on his face.

Trixie put her hands in the pockets of her jeans, elbows out to the side. Damn, she even rocked that simple move. "For a bit."

Boner scoffed. "Right. Spook ain't letting you out of his bed."

She shook her head, not acknowledging the statement, and I let it go.

"Hungry?"

She nodded.

"Let's go."

We walked up to the line where a house mouse gave me a sultry smile, and I swear to Christ, Trixie growled next to me. I pulled her against me and kissed her hard.

One thing this woman never had to worry about was me straying. There was no fucking way I was getting something I'd always wanted and throwing that shit away. Not happening.

"It's all good, babe."

She swiped at her swollen lips. "How do I know they won't poison me?"

I laughed deep and so hard my body shook. "Babe, they poison you, they poison us, and they wouldn't risk that shit."

She harrumphed and picked up a plate, eyeing the woman in front of her. Her name was Pony, and she'd been with us for a few months.

I lifted my chin to her, silently communicating for her to get the fuck out of there. She wasted no time darting off.

Trixie kept scanning the space, but I said nothing. I knew she was looking for Nanette.

We grabbed our food and joined the guys.

"So, how'd it go yesterday?" Stiff asked.

Trixie's eyes shot to mine. "You told them?"

"Babe, I tell them everything that impacts the club. Ya gotta know that."

Her shoulders sagged a bit in defeat, and I didn't like that shit one bit.

I turned toward her fully and continued in a lower tone, meant only for her. "Do I tell them what we do in bed? Fuck no. But, Trixie, if it puts my club on the radar, then I have to protect my family. This right here"—I motioned with my fork, encompassing the space—"is my family. I'd do anything for them, and they damn well know it. Just like you."

While she looked down at her food, I could see the small smirk on her lips. Fucking loved that.

I replayed what happened yesterday with the Colonel, and the air in the room turned as thick as I knew it would. Trixie came to full attention, noticing the change, as well.

I finished with, "That's why I need someone on Trixie when she's not here."

"On it," Dawg said. I knew he'd take care of everything. He was good about that.

"Son of a bitch is fucking crazy. He'd do it.", Boner said, looking at Trixie. "You've gotta be smart when you're not here."

Her eyes narrowed on him, and he lifted his hands in surrender.

"Not being a dick. I get that you can take care of yourself. What I'm saying is you know better than anyone the type of man the Colonel is. He touches you, and we all go after him."

Surprising me, Trixie reached over and grabbed my hand, squeezing it. She felt it, felt the way my boys were going to protect her. Fuck yes.

All she did was nod. No snappy comebacks, no sass. Just a simple movement to let Boner know she understood.

I squeezed her hand. "What do you have planned for today?"

"Later, I need to go to Sirens, but other than that, I don't know."

Before I could speak, Bosco shouted, "Rematch. Poker."

Trixie went solid.

"No tests or any of that shit. Just pure poker, even if you are a shark," Bosco teased.

She relaxed a bit and smarted back, "You do realize I'll beat the shit out of you."

Bosco full-out laughed. "Oh, fuck that. You were lucky." He didn't believe that for a damn second, but he was playing along.

I had to admit, I loved fucking seeing my woman be so damn accepted by my brothers. It meant the fucking world to me.

THREE HOURS LATER, I SAT WITH Trixie on my lap, which she tried to protest, but I wasn't having it. I watched as my woman annihilated my brothers in poker. One hand after another, she wiped each of the brothers out. The best part of the whole thing was her fucking laughter after winning the hands. She impressed me so damn much, not just at poker, but the way she could read people. I needed to ask her what the hell she saw each time to know.

The last round was between Trixie and Worm. "All in," Trixie called to Worm's nod. He'd always been quiet, ever since joining seven years ago. He did his time earning his patch and was a man I trusted. The cards were dealt, and neither of the two gave anything off. They only stared at one another.

Every so often, I'd feel Trixie's inner thigh muscles jump, but that was it. Finally, the cards were laid down.

"Fuck me!" Trixie yelled, sitting back into me in defeat. "Two damn pairs and he still beat me with three of a kind." A small smile played on her lips, and I knew, as much as she didn't like losing, she was happy. Therefore, I was happy.

"YOU KNOW, IF YOU DO THIS"—Trixie pushed some buttons on my computer in my office at the shop—"then it'll add all of that for you, and you don't have to sit there with your calculator and do it."

I knew this but was double-checking the computer. I wouldn't tell her this, though. She was feeling like part of the club, getting more involved over the last couple of days. She even gave me some tips on keeping inventory at the shop tight, which I fully admit I didn't know and ended up being a huge help. Not only did she explain it to Stiff, but she explained it to the others who were implementing it.

She told me late the other night that she didn't feel like she was doing anything here at the club other than eat and lay around before going to work. I'd explained to her how she'd already helped so fucking much in the shop, and she liked that. I fucking liked that. Liked having her in my space.

"Thanks, babe."

That got me a smile.

Her eyes fought back and forth with something, and then she leaned down and kissed my cheek. I grabbed the back of her hair, clutching it tight and deepening the kiss.

A knock came on the door, but I didn't pull away as it opened.

"Spook!" my mother's voice called.

Trixie stilled, pulling away from me and looking at my mother.

"Hey, Mom," I said, not moving one inch from Trixie.

My mother's eyes narrowed on Trixie, but her words were meant for me. "Didn't know you *played* in the office," she said in a clipped tone, and Trixie's back went ramrod straight.

My mother was referring to Trixie as a house mouse, and I didn't fucking like that one bit.

"Mom, this is Trixie. She's no fucking mouse."

Trixie's eyes sliced into me in warning. I just shrugged.

My mother didn't look convinced. "Whatever. I need to talk to you."

The way she dismissed Trixie did not sit right with me, either. No way in fuck would I allow my mother to disrespect her. Trixie would soon have the spot in this club that my mother had held for many years. I wouldn't allow her to diminish that power.

I pulled Trixie to my side as she tried to pull away. Not a fucking chance.

"Anything you say, you can say in front of Trixie."

"I don't think so," she said dismissively, pissing me way the fuck off.

"Mother," I snapped, and her eyes grew wide like saucers. "This is Trixie Lamasters. You remember her from my high school days."

My mother's mind started working, and as soon as it clicked inside her head, she stared at me in shock. She knew all about my father's side business, even turned her head when my father *broke in* the girls. She'd accepted everything as it was, never stepping on my father's toes. I never knew if she found out my bullet killed my father, though, and I'd never tell her. Sad thing was, the trust in my mother was teetering.

"Yeah, you get it now. Trixie's mine. Don't fucking dismiss that, Mother, or you won't like what happens."

"Spook," Trixie whispered.

I shook my head. I didn't need to hear that I was being disrespectful to my mother or any other shit that was bound to come out of her mouth. I did catch, though, that she called me Spook. She'd been doing that more when the guys were around or at the shop, leaving *Cade* for our time alone. Fucking loved that, too.

"Finally grew some balls and went after her," my mother said condescendingly, making my veins boil.

Trixie wrapped her arm around mine. Loved how she knew I was about to blow and tried to calm me. While she did to a point, I was pissed as hell at my mother.

"You need to watch yourself and shut the fuck up before I ban you from here altogether."

She waved her hand dismissively at me. "My boys won't get rid of me," she said with confidence, yet she had no fucking clue.

One word from me, and she would be done. The brothers only put up with her shit because she was my mother. If she kept giving them shit, they'd be in line with any decision I made.

The muscles in my arm bunched, and Trixie squeezed me to the point of pain, bringing me back from my fury.

"What do you need?" I barked.

This time, she lost a little color. "I don't wanna talk about it in front of an audience," she said snippily.

"Maybe I should …" Trixie started, but I pinned her with a look that shut her up quick. I didn't know what I looked like, but it did the trick. She didn't have a smartass comment. No, instead, she zipped her lips, turning her attention back my mother.

"No. Anything you need to say, say it." My words were short and clipped. I felt the anger radiating off my skin.

"I …" She sighed. "I went to Fox's table."

My anger turned into downright rage and contempt. She fucking did not. That was not what I expected her to say, especially after the lecture I had given her. The trust teetered over into nothingness.

"What!" I roared, trying to break away from Trixie and step toward my mother, but she held me to her, not releasing me. Sure, I could have made her, but I didn't. Instead of wringing my mother's fucking neck, I talked. "You owe him, you'll be on your back."

Trixie watched the exchange with vivid fascination. I remembered she didn't have a mother, so she probably didn't get that I was at my end with mine.

My mother reached into her large, black bag and pulled out an envelope. "I got you your money back. It'll be the last time I go. I'm giving it up," she said, holding out the envelope and stepping closer.

I took it from her and opened it as Trixie released me, noting quite a bit of cash there.

"You went to the table that I told you to stay the fuck away from to bring me this?" Normal people would probably be grateful to have their money back, but I wasn't "normal." I couldn't fucking believe she went back there after putting my club through shit to clean up her mess.

Trixie didn't know the whole story, and I was sure the little bit she was getting from this conversation wouldn't fill her in.

My mother stumbled. "I … I thought you'd be happy I got your money back."

Time to clue Trixie in.

"No, Mother," I clipped. "What if you fucking lost? Would you be coming to me to bail you out … again? I told you—no, I fucking ordered you to stay away from the tables, and you fucking did whatever the hell you wanted like always." I tossed the money back at her. "I'm fucking done with this shit. I'm done cleaning up your mess when you don't give a flying shit about me or my brothers. You take this money. It's the fucking last bit you're getting from me or the club. I tried to get through to you, but you don't get it, so I'm cutting you off. No more money from the club, no more support. None of us are getting you out of trouble."

Trixie took a deep breath, and my mother's face turned almost green. I didn't like this shit. I didn't like having to do it. But I'd warned her, and once again, she didn't listen.

"You can—"

"Six months You prove to me and the club you're turning shit around, then we'll talk. Once—just once—you go to Fox during that time, and we will cease to exist to you. Got me?"

My mother nodded, and a tear rolled down her cheek. I wouldn't let it affect me again. I needed to protect my club, my life, and Trixie's.

"I'm sorry, Spook," she said softly, and for the first time, I actually believed her.

She turned and walked out the door.

Trixie's gaze penetrated mine as I breathed deep, bringing myself down from the anger. I didn't like doing that to my mother, but it had to be done.

"Why did you do that?" Trixie asked quietly.

I moved around to my desk chair and sat with a thud. I rubbed my hands over my face and head. "Couldn't do it anymore. She's always bringing shit to me, and it was enough. She's dragging not only me, but my brothers into it. It had to stop, and the only way to do that was to pull the rug out from underneath her."

"But you didn't really. You let her keep whatever was in that envelope."

I smiled at my girl. She was so damn observant.

"Yeah, couldn't send her out empty."

She came around to my chair and wedged herself between my legs. I brought my hands instantly to her hips.

"You're a good man, Cade Baker." She smiled. "I mean, Spook." She bent down and kissed me. For the first time, I let her lead, and it was spectacular.

SEVENTEEN

TRIX

"**H**ELLO," I ANSWERED THE PHONE, already knowing Jett was on the other end.

I was sitting in Cade's house after finishing cleaning the pit. I told myself I wasn't going to do it, but after being in his space for days, it was driving me crazy. I couldn't take the mess another moment, so I gave in and cleaned.

"We have a problem."

It was early afternoon, and I'd told Jett I wouldn't be in until later. Truth be told, I really liked spending time with Cade and his brothers. They were funny, made me laugh, and made me feel like I belonged, something I had never thought I would feel.

"What?" I sat up, ready for whatever she was going to hit me with. It could be about anything.

"We're down bouncers and bartenders. Five of them. I even called the backups to the backups, and none of them could come in. Some shit about a big game on TV. I told them to get their asses to work, and they just laughed. Don't know how we're gonna open like this."

Fuck!

Cade strode in the door, and my breath caught at the sight of him. These past few days, I'd really gotten to see him, the man, and I had to admit I liked what I saw. No, scratch that. I loved what I saw.

"Alright. I'll get it taken care of. I'll be there in ten," I told her then clicked off.

"What?" Cade asked as I got up from the couch and searched for my shoes.

"I'm down five guys at the club. Some game's on, and they all bailed on me. I gotta figure this shit out."

"Babe, it's called the Super Bowl, and no wonder they called in."

I rolled my eyes. "Men and their shit." I laced both shoes and went looking for my bag.

"What are you gonna do?"

The rock hit my gut. "I don't have a clue. Second string was called, and they bailed, too, so maybe I can find some temps." Where there was a will, there was a way, right?

Cade pulled out his phone. "Round up the boys. Trixie needs us."

My head swung in his direction, my mouth agape. "What are you …?" I started, but was cut off by a pointer finger in the air.

"Sirens." He listened for a beat. "Yeah, I know." He chuckled and clicked the phone off.

"What did you just do, and what do you know?"

He walked up to me and pressed his hot body to mine. "I got you your third string, and Boner says you owe them. There is a big game on, after all."

My heart filled with something I wasn't familiar with, and I felt my throat begin to seize up. I'd never really been able to count on anyone in my life, and Vipers Creed was giving that to me. I felt it. I was scared of it, but it was there. It had always been there, under layers of bullshit that I didn't ever think I could come out of. But Cade pulled me out of it. I loved it. Loved this feeling.

For a week, I'd been in Cade's world, and it was undeniably sucking me in. Hell, Cade had sucked me in, and I was enjoying the ride.

We still hadn't heard anything from my father, and I really hoped he wouldn't do anything to me, but Cade wasn't taking any chances. He kept a guy on me all the time, rotating watches. After pissing me off for the first few days, I was able to let it go and just be. They were all fine except for Stiff. He talked and talked and talked. I didn't get shit done with him there. It would have been better had I just stayed home.

He also had this flirtation thing going on with Jett that I squashed, or at least, I liked to tell myself I had. He'd say something Stiff-ish, and she'd blush. Those were the only moments I got anything done.

Today, I had Lee. When I asked why he had a normal name, Cade had told me that the guys didn't get their road name until they were members. Lee was a prospect trying to get into the club, therefore, no name. When I looked at Lee compared to the other guys in the club, I didn't see it. He was a kid. Cade told me Lee was twenty-two, but he looked so much younger than that. It had to be his face. I wanted to tell him some of my zit secrets, but I felt like an ass even bringing it up. I didn't know how he felt about it, and it wasn't my place.

Lee was quiet, either sitting in my office or hanging out just outside the door. He'd switch things up and check his phone every so often while I worked.

My phone beeped with a message.

See you at home, Cade wrote.

Home. Sure, I had my house, but it never really felt like a home. Not until I moved to Cade's had I felt that. Like I belonged. Like I was part of something bigger than me and Sirens. A family, a life.

Leaving in a bit, I replied.

Jett popped in the door, eyeing Lee sitting on the couch. "Everything's cleaned up. I'm heading out."

"Night, Jett."

"Don't stay too late."

I shook my head. "I'm just finishing these numbers. Then I'm ready to go."

"Night," she said, shutting the door.

Thirty minutes later, I rose from my chair, stretching. "Let's go," I told Lee, who jumped up, looking more than happy to get out of here.

We walked out of the building toward my car, Lee right at my back, when a loud bang echoed throughout the night's sky, and Lee's body collapsed to the ground in a heap. I had my gun out and ready, but before I could shoot, a rag was placed over my face and the gun knocked out of my hands.

I struggled hard, flailing my arms and scratching at any part of skin I could reach, but the person behind me was stronger. I didn't know what was on the rag, but it smelled funny, and within moments, I was out cold.

My head filled with a cloudy, dense fog that I couldn't shake. Even with my eyes open, a filmy haze covered them, making everything blurry. Voices were muffled, as if I were under water, sinking. I thought I recognized one, but couldn't tell for sure.

Too hard to think.

I attempted to pull my arms up, but they were immediately halted by something. The hard, cold, heavy attachments clinked like metal. Even straining to move them, my muscles were so weak, so lethargic I couldn't. I tried my legs, and the same thing happened.

A hard surface pressed against my back as the cool air of the room cascaded over my skin, my nipples, my stomach… Oh God, was I naked?

I opened my mouth, wanting to scream as deep panic set in. Unfortunately, nothing came out except air. Even that took more effort than I had in me.

Placing the pieces of the puzzle together, I couldn't make heads or tails out of anything.

Heat at my side had me turning in that direction, only to see a fuzzy, black figure. I squinted then blinked, trying to get the focus to come back, but nothing. Not a damn thing.

"Hello, darlin'. Welcome to hell."

I blacked out.

I AWOKE TO A MALE VOICE saying, "Maybe I gave her too much."

Everything came back to me in a rush. I feared what whoever this was had given me. I was so damn cold my fingers felt like they would fall off at any time.

I opened my eyes and wished I hadn't. I was in a large, white room with bright florescent lights reminding me of a hospital, but the room was bare.

I pulled on my arms but nothing happened.

"See, she's awake."

I looked towards the end of whatever hard surface I was lying on and blinked rapidly. I was sure my eyes were playing tricks on me.

"Worm?" No, he wouldn't betray Cade or the club, would he?

"Ah, you remember my name." He gave me a wicked smile. It was more words than I had ever heard him say at once.

"So, you're the one." I followed the deep voice, and my heart completely stopped. Cobalt blue eyes stared back at me with the same dark hair as Cade's, but this wasn't him. "My son has good taste." He licked his gross, flaky lips.

Fear like no other pelted me.

"You're dead," I said stupidly.

He laughed, but it wasn't humorous. "Nah. It's amazing what money can buy."

I shook my head. This wasn't right. I had to be dreaming or something.

"No, Cade said he shot you dead."

His face turned hard. "The little fucker thought he did. Had Moose over there"—he nodded somewhere behind me that I couldn't see—"get me the fuck out of there. Money bought me my life back."

"I don't get it."

"You're a fucking woman; you're not supposed to get it." He gripped my hair hard and pulled my head taut, ripping strands of it from my scalp. "You, little bitch, are a means to an end. Spook comes, I take what's mine. I've got a great buyer for you. Loves whips and knives."

He was going to sell me? Oh, God. Whips and knives? Holy shit. I tried again to move my arms and legs. The panic was more than I could take.

"Worm's gonna give you a little taste of what's in store for you while we wait for my boy to figure out where you are. I give him about thirty minutes after I place the call. So you get a half-hour of fun with Worm here." He released my hair, and my head thudded on the hardness beneath me.

My eyes moved back to Worm. "But I played cards with you. You were nice to me."

He shrugged. "You're just pussy. That's what all women are."

I couldn't wrap my brain around all of this, but I didn't have time to.

A sharp pain came to my shin. I screamed, lifting my head to see what was happening.

Worm stood with a blade in his hand and blood dripping down my leg.

Oh, God.

EIGHTEEN

SPOOK

"NEITHER TRIXIE OR LEE ARE answering their goddamned phones." I charged through the clubhouse with Boner on my heels. "Fuck!"

"Calm down, brother. You don't know if something happened," Boner tried reassuring me. I felt like something had, though. The hair on the back of my neck was standing to attention, and a wave of unease settled in my gut. Something was wrong, way wrong.

"Stiff!" I yelled over at the bar.

He came to full attention. "What's goin' on?"

"Trixie and Lee are off radar. Get ahold of Dawg and get eyes. Find out what the fuck is going on."

"On it." He pulled out his phone as he followed us through the clubhouse, out to the lot, and on our bikes.

Pulling up to Sirens, we saw a body lying in the fucking parking lot. I pulled up closer, and fucking shit, it was Lee.

I parked the bike quickly, hopping off and going straight to him. I checked his breathing, nothing. Blood was splattered on the ground near his chest. Fucking hell.

"He's gone. Fuck. Call Dawg!" The death of this man rested on my fucking shoulders.

A chill ran down my back. I grabbed my phone, found the number, and hit the green button.

"What?" was answered on the other end.

"Where did you fucking take her?" I growled into the phone.

He said nothing in response.

Stiff came up to me. "Video. Covered her mouth with a rag and threw her in a dark SUV. No plates."

"You fucking son of a bitch, where in the fuck is Trixie!" I clenched the phone so hard the plastic cracked.

"I don't have her," her father claimed, yet I didn't fucking buy it for one second.

"Bullshit! You're the only motherfucker who's threatened her! I know you have her! Give her to me!" Every word was yelled with anger so fierce I couldn't contain it.

He was not taking Trixie from me. No fucking way.

"I'm telling you I don't have her. I never intended on taking her, you dick."

"I don't fucking believe you." I moved to my bike, not knowing where the hell I was going or who I was going to.

"Fine, don't believe me. Where the fuck are you?"

"Sirens, asshole!"

"Me and my guys will be there in ten." The line disconnected.

I'd fucking kill the motherfucker with my bare hands.

"Fucking shit!" I yelled into the dark night.

In any other situation, I'd be calm as could be, but not with Trixie. No fucking way with her.

"Brother, get your shit together." Boner came up, putting his hand on my back.

I brushed him off. I was too high strung and losing my shit.

"Spook, you're not doing her any good like this. Calm. The fuck. Down."

He was right, but fuck.

"Dawg?" I asked Stiff.

"He says they went right, but he lost them. No fucking clue, man."

I ripped my fingers through my hair.

"Got guys coming to get Lee," Stiff added.

Fucking hell. I looked down at the ground and took some serious deep breaths. I needed to think. I needed to clear my fucking head, or all of this was going to shit fast.

My phone rang. *Unknown caller.* I answered it, thinking it was dickhead Colonel.

"What!" I barked.

"Now, son, is that any way to greet your father?"

I stilled. What the fuck …? But the voice … Fucking hell, this couldn't be happening. Fifteen years raced through my thoughts, along with the memory of when the bullet had gone through his chest.

It took me a moment, but I had to get my shit together quickly.

"Speaking from the grave, Pusher?" I questioned, saying his road name specifically so the two men next to me would hear.

Their eyes grew wide.

"Oh, boy, you never did learn, did you?"

"I put your fucking ass in the ground." I paced the area. This couldn't be happening. This was like TV shit or something, not real life. I fucking shot him. He was dead.

"You put a man in the ground, but it wasn't me."

"Tell me what the fuck is going on," I demanded, and then it hit me.

He had Trixie. That motherfucker had her! Fucking hell!

I mouthed those same words to Boner and Stiff, who were punching things in on their phones.

"Well, son, you tried to kill your own blood. I've been waiting for just the right opportunity, and low and behold, the little bitch you fucked in high school shows up at your door."

My blood boiled at his description of Trixie.

"See, you thought you were smart, but boy, I'm fucking smarter."

"Where is she?"

"I'm not telling you."

Screams echoed in the background. Holy fuck, they were Trixie's. Oh, fucking shit.

"Stop fucking hurting her!" I screamed, unable to contain myself.

"Nah, she's a fun toy. You know exactly where I am. And, boy, I have cameras everywhere. You bring anyone with you, I'll gut her." The phone went dead.

It took everything in me not to throw the fucking phone across the lot.

I searched my mind from when he was alive, and he was right. I knew exactly where he had her. The same goddamned place where he took all the *girls* to *train* them.

"The warehouse," I told Boner.

His face went hard. "You're fucking shitting me."

"Call the boys. It needs to be quiet. Dawg needs to hack into the feed—there are cameras everywhere—and we need more fire power."

"On it." Stiff got busy just as two black SUVs pulled up, and the Colonel jumped out.

"Who has my daughter?" His tone was strong and resolute.

"My fucking father."

He flinched. It was the most expression I'd ever seen from him.

"You're fucking driving. Bikes are too loud, and cameras are on site."

"Get in."

We did so with Stiff still on the phone.

The Colonel gave directions to the man at the wheel as we darted through traffic. He knew exactly where we were going, but in giving over the business to the Colonel, he didn't want the space. I sure as shit wouldn't use it. So, it remained unused, or so I thought.

We stopped, but Dawg hadn't been able to cut the feed yet. If we didn't get it, then I was going in by my damn self.

"Firepower?" I asked.

"Back," the Colonel answered.

I reached behind me, grabbing several guns. I had my knife in my boot along with a small gun in the other. I strapped on the other weapons. My father was not fucking hurting or selling my woman. No way in hell.

Her screams echoed through my head.

"I'm fucking going in. Once you get the feed cut, come." *If* they could cut it. "If not, wait ten minutes and come in firing."

"You think you should go in without a man at your back?" Boner asked.

While I knew once a-fucking-gain he was right, I couldn't take the risk.

"He wants me, Boner, not Trixie."

"He's not selling my fucking kid," the Colonel said with absolute certainty.

"No, he's fucking not."

My head cleared with determination. My father would check for weapons. I put the guns down but left the knife. If I showed up packing, it wouldn't end well for either of us. Worse, I didn't know who in the hell was with him.

"I'll deal with it. Hold it steady," the Colonel ordered.

While I didn't do well with orders, I would take this one.

"Take the SUV behind us. My guys will get in this one."

I hopped out and switched SUVs. It was time to get my girl.

I pulled up to the warehouse, and old memories bombarded me. I fucking hated this place. I should have burnt it to the damn ground. I had been a kid but knew the shit that went on here was wrong. Way wrong, and it needed to end.

As soon as I parked, two bulky men came at me. I got out of the car and held my hands up.

"Turn the fuck around," asshole one said.

I did, and they searched me, not finding the knife. My father failed on his training.

"Move," asshole two said, pushing me. It took everything in my power not to fucking punch him in the teeth.

Asshole one opened the door. The smell of alcohol and fear penetrated the air. It was like fifteen years hadn't passed, and I was right back in the hell where all of this had started.

I walked down the hallway, guns at my back. I had no doubt I wasn't coming out of here alive, but I'd make damn sure Trixie did. I knew exactly where I was going, and I fucking hated it.

I turned toward the door just as one of the assholes pushed my back. I ignored it because my eyes landed on my fucking father.

There he was, flesh and fucking bone. His dark hair had spots of gray, and his face had lines of age. His eyes … I fucking hated that we shared the same eyes. They gleamed as he saw me.

"My son! You came." He clapped his hands together in excitement.

My eyes caught movement off to the left. Holy fucking shit. Stacy the house mouse who hurt Trixie and another woman I didn't recognize were in full-out, small metal cages. There were no other words to use to describe them, because they were literally wire frames that had held dogs at one time.

Tears streamed down the other girl's face, whereas Stacy had a sense of void in her eyes.

I trained my attention back on my father.

"Where is she?"

He pointed into *the room*.

Fuck, I hated that place. I never wanted to go back inside there in my life.

"She's where she should be."

That burned my veins.

A scream came from the door, and I made a move to go, but one of the assholes behind me pushed a gun to my head.

"You see? You do this my way." My father nodded to the guy. "Escort him in so he can see our handy work."

I moved inside the doorway, and my eyes landed on Trixie. Inside, I wept for her as I boiled over in fury.

The words whore and slut were carved into her stomach and chest, and her blood dripped onto the floor. She was tied to the table by her hands and feet, no doubt in pain from the cuts. I just hoped that was all they had done to her.

Her eyes were frantic when she saw me.

"Nice of ya to finally show up," Worm said from the corner.

That motherfucker!

"You were working for my father?" How in the fuck had I missed that one? "I'll fucking gut you."

"Not before I gut her." He held the knife, turning it around in his hand like he had all the time in the world.

Trixie breathed out deep, and my gaze went to hers. Our eyes connected, and

I mouthed "*trust me.*" She nodded, tears staining her cheeks. I didn't have a fucking clue how I was going to swing this, but I was going to figure it out and fast.

I looked at my father. "You sick son of a bitch, you're still doing this shit?"

He chuckled, but it wasn't a happy one.

He moved over to Trixie, running his hand down her face, and she flinched away, amusing him.

"Of course, and this one will be fun to break." Absolutely fucking not. "Thought you got rid of me, did ya?"

Yes, I fucking did. How I screwed this shit up, I'd never know.

"How?" I asked, trying to stall for time.

Fuck, I didn't think I had the ten minutes to spare. I needed a plan B, and that was going to be hard. Take the guns from the assholes behind me then take out my father and Worm. Easy, right? Four against one was not good odds, but if shit didn't get sorted soon, I was fighting our way out of here.

In walked a guy who had taken off from the club after I'd shot my father. The asshole had said he couldn't stand by and let me run the show after killing off our president, and here he fucking was. Not only that, but that seriously fucked up my odds.

"Moose?"

"In the flesh. Nice to see ya, Spooky," he teased with a chuckle.

I still didn't understand how all of this came together, but I needed some answers.

"How in the fuck are you alive?" I asked my father.

Trixie fisted her hands. I was happy to see she was ready to fight, because that was what this would be. I needed her on fire and ready to go.

"Medicine. A guy I sold whores to owed me a favor." Fucking hell.

"So, for fifteen years, you've been healing?"

The asshole behind me dug the gun into my back, but I didn't move.

"No, I've been setting up my business, getting it back on track. After you gave it to that dickhead, I had a lot to rebuild."

"Does the Colonel know you're stealing his business?"

Keeping him talking right now was the best way to make time to figure out a way out of this mess.

But when he said, "He's fucking next," it shocked me, because the Colonel was the baddest of the bad, and if my father thought he'd take him out, he was even more delusional than I thought. And fuck, I thought he was seriously delusional before. It did help, though, that Trixie's father wasn't in bed with my old man, even if the shit he did was despicable.

"I'll be sure you pay for giving my business away. Maybe I'll let every guy in this room fuck this little bitch while you watch." He reached for her.

"Get your fucking hands off her!" Rage filled me, and I let the adrenaline fuel me.

Quick as a flash, I reached behind me, throat punching one of the assholes then kicking the other. I was able to get my arm around asshole one and snap his neck before I picked up the gun and shot asshole two in the head.

I turned the gun to Worm and shot him between the eyes. I wished I could have sliced him up while he was living, but time was of the essence.

Three down; two to go.

When my father took a gun out and placed it at Trixie's temple, I stopped.

"Put the fucking gun down," my father growled.

Reluctantly, I did.

"Kick it to me." I did as he pushed the gun harder into Trixie's head.

She didn't whimper, even though I knew she had to be in some serious pain. The steel of her spine was coming through, my feisty strong woman. Fuck, I loved her.

Moose came up, and while I blocked the punch to the face, I missed the one to the gut. It hurt, but I held myself strong. The hit to my back had me down on one knee.

"Now that's better, son," my father said as Moose stepped away. "I think we need to give my boy here a little show for killing my men. Get a bottle," he ordered.

Moose left the room then came back, bringing a beer bottle in. My father held it by the neck then smashed it, breaking just the end off, leaving shards of glass poking out at every angle. Fuck.

"I think I need to tear this bitch up from the inside out. What do you think,

Moose?"

Moose chuckled. "Fuck, yeah."

That shit was not happening.

I charged my father, hitting him in the gut. We both went down, the bottle falling to the floor and rolling away.

Moose attacked me from the back as I pummeled my fists into my father's face. I ignored Moose and let all the rage I had out on my father.

A shot to the kidneys had me wincing, giving them both the edge they needed.

Moose grabbed me under my arms and held me fast while my father rose and began punching, each one becoming more brutal than the last. I was losing. Horribly. But I kept fighting with everything I had. I fought for all I was worth.

My energy waned, the pain intense, but I was doing this for Trixie. I had to get her out.

My foot connected with my father's knee, and he buckled. I took that opportunity to throw my head back as hard as I could and heard bones crack. Moose staggered back.

I grabbed a gun from the floor and shot him square in the eye. Then I held the gun on my father as he rose by the door.

I had no doubt he had a plan B. He always did, but this time, he wasn't leaving here alive.

Movement by the door got my attention.

"Fucking shit," Boner said.

"Untie her," I told him as the Colonel entered the room.

He sighed; but otherwise, he didn't have any reaction to his daughter being naked and bleeding. Asshole.

Boner pulled a trembling Trixie into his arms. I wanted to be the one holding her, so I ended the game.

"This time, I'll make sure you're in the grave." I shot my father in the head four times in rapid succession. When his body fell, I went up to him and kept shooting into his brain.

"He's dead," the Colonel proclaimed in a bored manner, his arms crossed.

I squeezed off two more rounds. "Just making sure."

I moved to Boner, the pain in my body intense. I was pretty sure I had a cracked rib or three, and something was wrong with my kidneys.

Trixie's eyes met mine and tears fell, rolling down her cheeks. "I trust you," she said, which was better than *I love you* to me.

I went to pick her up, but pain speared up my arm to my shoulder. Don't know what the fuck I did there. Shit.

"I can't carry you, babe. Boner needs to, but I'll hold you when we get to the car." I turned to Stiff. "Get the girls in the cages out."

He nodded.

Trixie's eyes drifted outside the door. "Nanette," she whispered.

Oh, fucking hell. How long had she been gone now? Days? Weeks? Fuck, I hated to think of all the shit my father could have done with her in five minutes, let alone that long.

"Guess we found her," Boner said.

Nanette cried from her cage, "Trixie, I'm so sorry." She was an utter mess, blood and other fluids coating her naked body. It was despicable.

Trixie raised her head from Boner's grip. "It's alright. The guys will get you out of here. Trust them to take care of you."

Nanette continued to sob, while Stacy had the blankest look on her face. She was somewhere else, not in her mind, and fuck if that didn't piss me off.

"The money," Nanette said, which I thought was bizarre considering she was in a fucking cage, but my Trixie didn't skip a beat.

"Clear," Trixie said, and Nanette continued to weep.

"Let's get the fuck out of here. Now," I ordered, needing to be on a different fucking planet from this place.

We loaded into the car, and I held my girl. Her body shook, but she had two blankets on her, and I was hoping it would help.

I turned around for just a moment to see that fucking warehouse finally go up in flames.

NINETEEN

SPOOK

BONER CARRIED TRIXIE INTO MY room at the clubhouse where Needles, our club doctor, waited. He was an older man the club used over the years. He always came when called, didn't ask questions, and did whatever was needed to be done. Exactly what we needed.

His eyes darted from Trixie to me, and I nodded my head toward her. It was always her. No matter fucking what, she came before me ... always.

Boner laid her on the bed where she continued to shiver. I had Boner crank the heat up in the SUV, but along with my body heat and the blankets, it hadn't helped.

She groaned as I sat on the bed next to her and gripped her hand. She hung on with every bit of strength she had inside her. She was so damn strong, so seeing her hurt was like taking a blade directly to my heart.

Needles had an area set up with gauze and other doctor shit, but as he moved to the side of the bed, Trixie began trembling more fiercely.

"Trixie, this is Needles, our doctor. He's gonna take a look at you."

Fear flamed in her eyes like a wildfire. "No," she choked out, moving next to me and groaning as she did. Fuck, I hated this.

"Baby." I touched the side of her face, and her beautiful green eyes focused only on me. "You're safe. I've got you."

She breathed out harshly, but it wasn't from disbelief. It was from relief.

"He's gonna have to stitch you up."

I could see the moment her determination came back into her body, her shoulders relaxing a touch as she batted away the tears.

"That's my girl." I looked at Needles. "What do you need?"

"I've got it all. Let me check her out."

I nodded then turned back to Trixie. "I've gotta remove the blankets. I know you're cold, but I'll warm you up as soon as I can."

"I'm good, Cade," she said softly. I was fucking ecstatic her tone didn't have fear lacing it.

"Yeah, baby, you are." I gave her a reassuring smile then turned back to Needles. "Do what you've gotta do."

He stepped up to Trixie. "Hey, Trixie. I'm just gonna take a look and see what we've got here."

"Okay," she told him.

He turned to me. "You wrap her in this while she was still bleeding?"

"Yeah."

"Fuck," he grumbled, turning back to Trixie. "The blanket probably dried the blood, so when I pull it off, it's gonna hurt."

Trixie's eyes closed then slowly opened. "Just do it," she told him, licking her lips.

"It's like a band-aid. I'm gonna do it gently but quick."

She just nodded as he took the blanket off. He was right. Parts of it were stuck to the wounds on my girl's beautiful skin, but she didn't cry out. The only thing she did was close her eyes and bite her bottom lip. My tough girl.

"Fucking hell," Needles said, and Trixie's face turned toward me.

"It's bad?" she whispered.

Yeah, it was fucking bad. The words etched into her skin made me want to kill my father all over again. And fucking Worm. I wanted to carve into his skin, dig out his eyeballs, and cut off his dick. Both those motherfuckers were gone, though. I'd made damn sure this time.

"Nothing that time won't heal."

I looked at Needles whose lip had turned up in disgust. When he focused on me, I could see it in his eyes. She'd have scars from this, with ones on the inside that wouldn't heal. Fucking hell.

"I'm gonna need your help, Spook." Needles handed me some wet gauze. Luckily, it was my left shoulder that hurt, and I was able to use my right. "Start getting all the blood off so I can get all the wounds cleaned."

The entire time I wiped Trixie, her eyes were shut tight, small drops of tears falling from the corners of them. She flinched a few times yet stayed solid. She didn't protest when Needles gave her a shot, saying it would make her more comfortable, along with a tetanus shot. She hardly moved as he stitched all the cuts on her body, which took so long I had thought she'd fallen asleep from the medicine. However, when Needles' gloves smacked as he took them off, her eyes fluttered open.

"Done?" she whispered.

"Yeah, Trixie." I didn't want to ask her this, but I had to. Needles needed to know everything. "Did ...?" I choked a bit on my words and cleared my throat. "Did they ... *touch* you?"

"No," she said in a sleepy voice. "Only the cuts and the bruises."

I brushed her hair back. "Good, baby." I looked at Needles. "Anything else you need to do?"

"No. Clean the wounds twice a day and add this cream." He handed me a tube. "Then redress it. She'll need sponge baths for a few days. Then she can do showers, but no baths, swimming, or hot tubs." Like we were going to go out and run to the damn beach. Whatever. "I need to check you now."

"Where are you hurt?" Trixie whispered, the medicine obviously making her ultra-drowsy, her words slurring.

"I'm fine," I lied. "Go to sleep. I'll be here when you wake up."

"Okay." She yawned and moments later, passed out.

"Now let's see what mess you've got yourself into, boy," Needles said.

After he twisted and turned my damn body, checking me out to the point I wanted to throat punch him, he said I had a strained muscle in my arm and shoulder.

My ribs weren't cracked, but bruised pretty good. He had me piss in a cup and determined that my kidneys were alright, but if I started pissing blood, I needed to call him. He gave me pain meds, along with Trixie's. Trixie also got antibiotics.

When he left, I stared down at the beautiful woman who I loved with everything inside of me.

A slight knock sounded on the door, and Boner poked his head in. "You alright?"

"Yeah, get a couple of the guys and help me change the sheets. Need to get the blood out of here."

He nodded as I wrapped a sheet around Trixie carefully.

It only took moments to change the bed, and Trixie didn't even stir as Stiff lifted her.

"What about the girls?" I asked Boner, Stiff, and Dawg.

"Stacy's a fucking mess. Nanette, she's scared to death, but appears to be okay." Boner grabbed the back of his neck, a frustrated look crossing his face. "I sent Needles to check them out."

"Good. That's good," I said, looking down at my girl. "I need to rest."

"You got it," Stiff said, taking one more look at Trixie's sleeping form then left the room, the others following suit.

I needed to touch her as I lay next to her, but I was afraid I'd rip open her wounds, so I grabbed her hand and held on tight.

"WHERE ARE WE GOING?" Trixie asked as I held her hand, walking through the illuminated lot of the clubhouse. It had been five days since she was hurt, and I wanted to get her out of the house.

"Surprise." I told her, opening the car door for her.

She gave me a soft smile, and I couldn't help leaning down to kiss her softly on the lips. Then she slowly sank down into the car seat, and I shut her door then ran around the car, hopping in the driver's seat. I had everything we needed in the trunk, ready to go.

Grabbing her hand, I held it the entire way, waiting for the moment when she would recognize where we were going. The streets were lit up by lights, and the pitch black night sky was calling to us. We wound around the roads that carried us higher and higher.

"Oh, my God," Trixie gasped, covering her mouth.

I grinned.

"You're taking me to Hollow Point?"

"Absolutely, baby." I gave her hand a squeeze. "I thought we could see the stars."

I parked the car turning completely toward her, seeing a tear roll down her cheek. I lifted my finger, wiping it from her flesh. "Why the tears, Trixie?"

Her gaze met mine. "This is absolutely perfect, Cade." Her smile radiated.

"I wanted to bring you to a place where my love for you began. You, me, looking up at the stars. You telling me all that shit about how stars are supposed to look like animals or whatever and me not giving a fuck about that, watching the animated look on your face while you told me, instead. Loving how your eyes lit up in excitement. I want you to show me the stars, Trixie," I whispered, lifting her hand and placing a kiss on it.

"Absolutely."

EPILOGUE

Four Months Later...

TRIX

I HAD NEVER BEEN AS TERRIFIED AS I was that day in that cold room. Not until I saw Cade had I begun to relax. I drawn on his strength because I'd been losing so much of mine.

When I told him I trusted him, I meant it with every fiber of my being. I loved him fifteen years ago, and I loved him in this moment.

Now, Cade sat at my head while a man named Blade tattooed ink into my skin. The needles poked into my skin, the buzz of the machine echoing throughout the small, enclosed room. The pricks really didn't hurt; I was pretty numb to it.

The external wounds had healed, leaving two very disturbing words etched into my flesh. I had put the ointment on them just like the doctor said in hopes it would allow the cuts to heal without marking my skin. It didn't work, and even though Cade said he didn't give a shit, I did.

There was no way I would be able to go through life, head held high, with those words from that dickhead etched into me, let alone have Cade see them every time

I was naked in front of him. No. That wasn't happening.

Getting a tattoo never really crossed my mind over the years. I thought they were hot as hell on men and pretty sexy on some of my girls at Sirens, but never had I thought of doing it myself. Not until this.

I'd been lying in his tattoo-covered arms when I came up with the idea. I got up from the bed that moment, grabbed my laptop, and began my search for ideas. Cade watched then joined me, holding me while I looked. It was the first time I felt like I was going to be okay.

"You good?" Blade asked, looking up from his needle, and I heard Cade shift.

"Yeah, keep going."

The buzzing started again, and I closed my eyes, letting this man wipe away the last physical reminders of that fateful night.

I'd checked in on Nanette, who was living with a girlfriend of hers. Her outside wounds had healed, but her internal ones seemed to keep her on edge. Cade told me the Vipers offered to help Nanette, which she accepted. At this point, it was mostly monetary, but I'd talked to her about seeing a professional. Last time I'd talked to her, she'd said she would think about it. That was the best I could do.

As far as Stacy, she'd disappeared one day, only to be found in a ditch off the highway a few days later. She'd never spoken to anyone, refusing to take any help from the Vipers. I hated to think about what had happened to her, and I was so damn sorry she'd had to go through it.

Cade admitted he carried Lee and Stacy's deaths on his shoulders. But like he'd told me, *It's part of the life, and I accepted that when I took the job as president.* It didn't mean that I couldn't comfort him in hopes of relieving some of that weight.

We all attended both of their services. Lee's parents were utterly distraught, and I felt that guilt. If Lee hadn't been with me that night, he'd still be alive. Cade told me to let him carry that load, but I'd never forget. Never forget either of them.

Stacy's service only consisted of the Vipers and myself. She had no family, and no friends had showed up. Sad didn't even cut it. I hoped she'd found her peace.

As I looked into the mirror four and a half hours later, tears came to my eyes. In that moment, I didn't give a shit if Blade or Cade saw me cry. No, because this moment was for me. The intricate design was outlined. It would take at least one more session, if not two, to get all the shading right.

Along my stomach and rib cage, up past my breasts was a dazzling mix of roses, stems with thorns and leaves that all interconnected, making one large piece on my body. Not fully shaded, it still looked beautiful. *I* looked beautiful. For the first time in four months, I felt it. I felt me.

I took back something that had been ripped from me. I erased it and survived it. I was alive and had a good man at my side. Happy didn't even sound like a good enough word for me at the moment, but I was running with it.

Cade stepped behind me, his chin coming to my shoulder. "You've always been the most gorgeous woman I've ever seen." He kissed my shoulder.

Shivers went down my spine, and a tingle started between my legs. My breathing picked up as I stared into Cade's eyes.

A snap of gloves in the room made me jump.

"On that note, keep it clean and put this on it." Blade handed me a tube of ointment. "And if you're gonna fuck, make sure not to get his sweat or any friction on it. Be creative." He winked at us both as he exited the room.

"Creative, huh?" I said to Cade as I pulled the shirt over my bare body, sans bra because of the tattoo. I figured that was going to be my norm for a while, and I was totally fine with that.

"I can do creative." Cade grabbed me, consuming me with a kiss that I'd missed and never wanted to end again. I needed this, needed him.

I threaded my fingers through his hair, pulling him as close to me as I could.

A cough came from the doorway, and we broke apart, looking at Blade who wore a wide smile on his face.

"Next client's comin' in."

"Fuck," Cade growled, grabbed my hand, and pulled us out the door then onto his bike, which I fucking loved riding, and took us home.

BONUS MESSAGE FROM THE COLONEL

You hate me. That's the way it's supposed to be.
Always remember, looks can be deceiving.

In The Red
Devil's Due MC Book 1
©2016 Chelsea Camaron

The event that shook one small town to its core was never solved. The domino effect of one person's crime going unpunished is beyond measure.

He's no saint.

Dover 'Collector' Ragnes rides with only five brothers at his back. Nomads with no place to call home, they never stay in one place too long. Together, they are the Devil's Due MC, and their only purpose is to serve justice their way for unsolved crimes everywhere they go.

She's not afraid to call herself a sinner.

Emerson Flint still remembers the loss of her elementary school best friend. She is all grown up, but the memories still haunt her of the missing girl. Surrounding herself with men at the tattoo shop, she never questions her safety. Her life is her art. Her canvas is the skin of others.

However, danger is at her door.

Will Dover overcome the history he shares with Emerson in time? Will Emerson lead him to the retribution he has always sought?

Love, hate, anger, and passion collide as the time comes, and the devil demands his due.

Prologue

I HANG MY HEAD AND SIT IN SILENCE. The television blares as strangers move about our house. Some of them are trying to put together a search party, and others are here with food and attempts to comfort. I want them all to go away. I want to scream or break something. I want them all to stop looking at me like I should be beaten within an inch of my life then allowed to heal, only to get beaten again. Do I deserve that?

Hell yes, I do, and more.

There is no reprieve from the hell we are in. I would sell my soul to the Devil himself if I could turn back time. Only, I can't.

The reporter's voice breaks through all of the clamor.

"In local news tonight, a nine-year-old girl is missing, and authorities are asking for your help. Raleigh Ragnes was last seen by her seventeen-year-old brother. According to her parents, her brother was watching her afterschool when the child wandered outside and down the street on her pink and white bicycle with streamers on the handlebars.

"She was last known to have her brown hair braided with a yellow ribbon tied at the bottom. She was in a yellow shirt and a black denim dress that went to her knees. She wore white Keds with two different color laces; one is pink, and one is purple.

"There is a reward offered for any information leading to the successful return of Raleigh to her home. Any information is appreciated and can be given by calling the local

sheriff's department."

The television seems to screech on and on with other reports as if our world hasn't just crumbled. My mom's sobs only grow louder.

God, I'm an ass. Raleigh was whining all afternoon about going to Emerson's house. Those two are practically inseparable. She had made the trip numerous times to the Flint's home at the end of the cul-de-sac, so I didn't think twice about her leaving.

Gretchen was here, locked in my room with me. My hand was just making it down her pants when I yelled at Raleigh through the door to just go, not wanting the distraction. My mind was only occupied with getting into Gretchen's pants.

Only, while I was making my way to home base, my little sister never made it to her friend's house. None of us knew until dinner time arrived and my sister never came home. The phone call to Emerson's sent us all into a tailspin.

While other families watch the eleven o'clock news to simply be informed, for my family, my little sister is the news.

~ Three weeks later ~

The television screeches once again. I thought the world had crumbled before, but now it's crushed and beyond repair. The reporter's tone is not any different than if they were giving the local weather as the words they speak crash through my ears.

"In local news tonight, the body of nine-year-old Raleigh Ragnes was found in a culvert pipe under Old Mill Road. Police are asking for anyone with any information to please come forward. The case is being treated as an open homicide."

In the matter of a month, my sister went from an innocent little girl to a case number, and in time, she will be nothing more than a file in a box. Everyone else may have called it cold and left it unsolved, but that's not who I am.

The domino effect of one person's crime going unpunished is beyond measure.

Chapter One
~Dover~

Giving up is not an option *for me ... It never has been.*
"There's a time and a place to die, brother," I say, scooping Trapper's drunk ass up off the dirty floor of the bar with both my hands under his armpits. "This ain't it."

It's a hole in the wall joint, the kind we find in small towns everywhere. It's a step above a shack on the outside, and the inside isn't much better: one open room, linoleum floor from the eighties. The bar runs the length of the space with a pair of saloon-style swinging doors closing off the stock room. We have gotten shit-faced in nicer, and we have spent more than our fair share of time in worse.

At the end of a long ride, a cold beer is a cold beer. Really, it doesn't matter to us where it's served as long as it has been on ice and is in a bottle.

"I'm nowhere near dying," he slurs, winking at the girl he has had on his lap for the last hour. She's another no name come guzzler in a slew of many we find throughout every city, town, and stop we make. "In fact, I'm not far from showing sweet thing here a little piece of heaven."

"Trapper." Judge, the calmest of us all, gets in his face. "She rode herself to oblivion until you fell off the stool. She's done got hers, man. Time to get you outta here so you can have some quality time huggin' Johnny tonight."

We all laugh as Trapper tries to shake me off. "Fuck all y'all. That pussy is mine tonight."

"Shithead, sober up. She's off to the bathroom to snort another line, and she won't be coming back for another ride on your thigh. Time to go, brother," Rowdy says sternly.

Trapper turns to the redheaded, six-foot, six-inch man of muscle and gives him a shit-eating grin. "Aw, Rowdy, are you gonna be my sober sister tonight?"

I wrap my arm around Trapper, pulling him into a tight hold. "Shut your mouth now!"

He holds up his hands in surrender, and we make our way out of the bar.

Another night, another dive. Tomorrow is a new day and a new ride.

Currently, we are in Leed, Alabama for a stop off. The green of the trees, the rough patches of the road—it all does nothing to bring any of us out of the haunting darkness we each carry.

We're nomads—no place to call home, and that's how we like it. The six of us have been a club of our own creation for almost two years now. We all have a story to tell. We all have a reason we do what we do. None of us are noble or honorable. We strike in the most unlikely of places and times, all based on our own brand of rules and systems.

Fuck the government. Fuck their laws. And damn sure fuck the judicial system.

Once your name is tainted, no matter how good you are, you will never be clean in the eyes of society. I'm walking, talking, can't sleep at night proof of it. Well, good fucking deal. I have learned society's version of clean is everything I don't ever want to be.

The scum that blends into our communities and with our children, the cons that can run a game, they think they are untouchable. The number of crimes outnumber the crime fighters. The lines between law abiding and law breaking blur every day inside every precinct. I know, because I carried the badge and thought I could be a change in the world. Then I found out everything is just as corrupt for the people upholding the law as those breaking it.

Day in and day out, watching cops run free who deserve to be behind bars more than the criminals they put away takes its toll. Everyone has a line in the sand, and once they cross it, they don't turn back. I found mine, and I found the brotherhood in the Devil's Due MC. Six guys who have all seen our own fair share of corruption in the justice system. Six guys who don't give a fuck about the consequences.

Well, that's where me and my boys ride in. No one's above the devil getting his due. We are happy to serve up our own kind of punishments that most certainly fit the crimes committed, and we don't bother with the current legal system's view of justice served.

We're wayward souls, damaged men, who have nothing more than vengeance on our minds.

"Fucking bitch, she got my pants wet," Trapper says, just realizing she really did get off on his thigh and left him behind. "You see this shit?" He points at his leg.

Trapper mad is good. He will become focused rather than let the alcohol keep him in a haze. He could use some time to dry up. He's sharp. His attention to detail saves our asses in city after city. However, things get too close to home when we ride to the deep south like this, and he can't shake the ghosts in the closets of his mind. At five-foot-ten and a rock solid one eighty-five, he's a force of controlled power. He uses his brain more than his brawn, but he won't back down in a brawl, either.

We help him get outside the dive bar we spent the last two hours inside, tossing beer back and playing pool. Outside, the fresh winter air hits him, and he shakes his head.

"It's not that cold," X says, slapping Trapper in the face. "Sober up, sucka."

Trapper smiles as he starts to ready his mind. As drunk as he is, he knows he has to have his head on straight to ride.

"Flank him on either side, but stay behind in case he lays her down. We only have four miles back to the hotel," I order, swinging my leg over my Harley Softail Slim and cranking it. The rumble soothes all that stays wound tight inside me. The vibration reminds me of the power under me.

Blowing out a breath, I tap the gas tank. "Ride for Raleigh," I whisper and point to the night sky. *Never forget,* I remind myself before I move to ride. My hands on the bars, twisting the throttle, I let the bike move me and lift my feet to rest on the pegs. As each of my brother's mount, I pull out, knowing they will hit the throttle and catch me, so I relax as the road passes under me.

We ride as six with no ties to anyone or anything from one city to the next. We have a bond. We are the only family for each other, and we keep it that way. No attachments, no commitments, and that means no casualties.

We are here by choice. Any man can leave the club and our life behind at any time. I trust these men with my life and with my death. When my time is called, they will move on with the missions as they come.

We don't often let one another drink and drive, but coming south, Trapper needed to cut loose for a bit. He may be drunk, yet once the wind hits his face, he will be solid. He always is.

At the no-tell motel we are crashing at, X takes Trapper with him to one of the three shit-ass rooms we booked while Judge and Rowdy go to the other. The place has seen better days, probably thirty years ago. It's a place to shit, shower, and maybe, if I can keep the nightmares away, sleep. I have never needed anything fancy, and tonight is no different.

I give them a half salute as they close their doors and lock down for the night.

Deacon heads on into our room. Always a man of few words and interaction, he doesn't look back or give me any indication that he cares if I follow or stay behind.

I give myself the same moment I take every night and stand out under the stars to smoke.

I look up. Immediately, I can hear her tiny voice in my mind, making up constellations all her own. Raleigh was once a rambunctious little girl. She was afraid of nothing. She loved the night sky and wishing upon all the stars.

Another city, another life, I wish it was another time, but one thing I know is that there is no turning back time. If I could, I would. Not just for me, but for all five of us.

I light my cigarette and take a deep drag. Inhaling, I hold it in my lungs before I blow out. The burn, the taste, and the touch of it to my lips don't ease the thoughts in my mind. Another night is upon us, and it's yet another night Raleigh will never come home.

The receptionist steps out beside me. She isn't the one who was here when we checked in earlier. When she smiles up at me, I can tell she has been waiting on us. Guess the trailer trash from day shift chatted up her replacement. Well, at least this one has nice teeth. Day shift definitely doesn't have dental on her benefit plan here.

"Go back inside," I bark, not really in the mood for company.

"I'm entitled to a break," she challenges with a southern drawl.

"If you want a night with a biker, I'm not the one," I try to warn her off.

"Harley, leather, cigarettes, and sexy—yeah, I think you're the one … for tonight, that is." She comes over and reaches out for the edges of my cut.

I grab her wrists. "You don't touch my cut."

She bites her bottom lip with a sly smile. "Oh, rules. I can play by the rules, big daddy."

I drop her hands and walk in a circle around her before standing in front of her then backing her to the wall. I take another drag of my cigarette and blow the smoke into her face. "I'm not your fucking daddy." I take another long drag. Smoke blows out with each word as I let her know. "If you wanna fuck, we'll fuck. Make no mistake, though, I'm not in the mood to chat, cuddle, or kiss. I'm a man; I'll fuck, and that's it."

She leans her head back, testing me.

"Hands against the wall," I order, and she slaps her palms against the brick behind her loudly.

Her chest rises and falls dramatically as her breathing increases. She keeps licking and biting her lips.

"You want a ride on the wild side?"

She nods, pushing her tits out at me.

"You wet for me?" I ask, and she giggles while nodding. "If you want me to get hard and stay hard, you don't fucking make a sound. That giggling shit is annoying as fuck."

Immediately, she snaps her mouth shut.

I yank her shirt up and pull her bra over her titties without unhooking it. Her nipples point out in the cold night air.

"You cold or is that for me?" I ask, flicking her nipple harshly.

"You," she whispers breathlessly.

I yank the waistband of her stretchy pants down, pulling her panties with them. Her curls glisten with her arousal under the street light.

With her pants at her ankles, I turn her around to face the wall.

"Bend over, grab your ankles. You don't speak, don't touch me, and you don't move. If you want a wild ride with a biker, I'm gonna give you one you'll never forget."

While she positions herself, I grab a condom from my wallet and unbutton my four button jeans enough to release my cock. While stroking myself a few times to get fully erect, part of me considers just walking away. However, I'm a man, and pussy is pussy. No matter what my mood, it's a place to sink into for a time.

Covering myself carefully, I spread her ass cheeks and slide myself inside her slick cunt.

The little whore is more than ready.

I close my eyes and picture a dark-haired beauty with ink covering her arms and a tight cunt made just for me. I can almost hear the gravelly voice of my dream woman as she moans my name, pushing back to take me deeper, thrust after thrust.

I roll my hips as the receptionist struggles to keep herself in position.

Raising my hand, I come down on the exposed globe of her ass cheek. "Dirty fucking girl." I spank her again. "I'm not your fucking daddy, but I'll give you what he obviously didn't." I spank her again and thrust. "Head down between your legs. Watch me fuck your pussy."

She does as instructed and watches as I continue slamming into her. Stilling, I reach down and twist her nipples as she pushes back on me.

Her moans get louder as I move, gripping her hips and pistoning in and out of her.

I slap her ass again. "I said quiet."

I push deep, my hips hitting her ass, and she shakes as her orgasm overtakes her.

"Fuck me!" she wails.

I slam in and out, in and out, faster and faster, until I explode inside the condom.

She isn't holding her ankles by the time I'm done. She's still head down, bent over with her back against the wall as her hands hang limply like the rest of her body, trembling in aftershocks.

Pulling out, I toss the condom on the ground and walk away, buttoning my pants back up.

"Collector," I hear X yell my road name from his doorway. "You ruined that one." He is smoking a cigarette. It's obvious he watched the show.

The noise has Judge coming to his door and giving me a nod of approval.

I look over my shoulder to see the bitch still hasn't moved. Her pussy is out in the air, ass up, head down, and she's still moaning. Desperate, needy, it's not my thing.

"I need a shower," I say, giving X a two finger salute before going into my own room. Deacon is already in bed and doesn't move as I go straight back to the shit-ass bathroom to clean up.

I wasn't lying. I smell like a bar, and now I smell the skank stench of easy pussy. I have needs, but I can't help wondering what it would be like to have to work for my release just once. It's not in my cards, though. Just like this town, this ride, and that broad, it's on to the next for me and my bothers of the Devil's Due MC.

Coming May 23, 2016
Amazon
http://amzn.to/1nGPebJ

About the Author

USA Today Bestselling author Chelsea Camaron is a small town Carolina girl with a big imagination. She is a wife and mom chasing her dreams. She writes contemporary romance, erotic suspense, and psychological thrillers. She loves to write blue-collar men who have real problems with a fictional twist. From mechanics to bikers to oil riggers to smokejumpers, bar owners, and beyond, she loves a strong hero who works hard and plays harder.

Chelsea can be found on social media at:
Facebook: www.facebook.com/authorchelseacamaron
Twitter: @chelseacamaron
Email: chelseacamaron@gmail.com

ABOUT RYAN MICHELLE

Ryan Michele has a huge obsession with reading, which only came to life after her best friend said she *had* to read *Twilight*. After reading that series, her entire world changed in the blink of an eye. Not only was she sucked into new worlds and all of the wonderful words authors put down on paper, she felt the urge to begin to write down the characters that played inside of her head.

When she's not reading or writing, she spends time taking care of her two children and her husband, enjoying the outdoors and laying in the sun.

Keep Up To Date with my Newsletter: http://tinyurl.com/
RyanMicheleNewsletter
Website : www.authorryanmichele.net
Facebook: www.facebook.com/AuthorRyanMichele
Twitter -- @Ryan_Michele

OTHER TITLES BY RYAN MICHELE

Made in the USA
Lexington, KY
02 November 2016